One Fine May

THE RAKE REVIEW
BOOK FIVE

COURTNEY MCCASKILL

First published in 2024 by Hazel Grove Books.

One Fine May Copyright © Courtney McCaskill, 2024.

Excerpt from *The Scot Who Made June Hot* Copyright © Fenna Edgewood, 2024.

Kindle ISBN: 978-1-63915-024-3

eBook ISBN: 978-1-63915-026-7

Paperback ISBN: 978-1-63915-025-0

This is a work of fiction. Names, principal characters, events, and incidents are the products of the author's imagination and have no factual basis. Any resemblance to actual persons, living or dead, or actual events is purely coincidental.

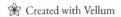 Created with Vellum

Chapter One

May 1820
London, England

As one of the most dissolute rakes in all of London, Evander Beauclerk was game to try almost anything. But today, he was doing something he absolutely *never* did.

Going over the ledgers of his father's insurance business.

This was a mark of how deeply he was dreading the conversation he was about to have with his father. He would do anything to distract himself.

Slouching in a leather wingchair in his father's study, Vander frowned as he scratched out the total in yet another column. He hated this sort of drudgework, and considering his father had insisted upon meeting at the ungodly hour of half-nine, he'd managed only three hours of sleep. Combined with the fact that his head was still pounding from the impressive volume of brandy he'd consumed the previous night, he wasn't adding up the numbers as effortlessly as he usually would.

But it was a good thing *someone* was double-checking these figures. It had never occurred to him that his father, from whom he had inherited his considerable mathematical acumen, would lose a step in his middle age. But judging by the fact that he had bungled the calculation in six out of the eight columns, it appeared the old man's mind was a shadow of its former glory.

The door swung open, and his father minced into the room with the tiny, precise stride Vander could have picked out from a mile away. Cedric Beauclerk pushed his spectacles up onto the bridge of his nose as he peered at his son. "Evander. Good, you're here."

Vander bit back a groan. His father was the only one who called him Evander. He was Vander to his friends, Beauclerk to most everyone else, and *Mister* Beauclerk in polite company... not that Vander found himself in polite company on anything resembling a regular basis.

It wasn't that Vander disliked his full name; it was more the way his father said it. He always managed to emphasize the first syllable, "EEE-Vander," in a way that made Vander feel like he was twelve years old and about to receive a paddling from the headmaster.

His father took his time arranging the file folder he'd brought with him on the oversized mahogany desk, then finally turned to his son.

"So. Evander. I imagine you know why I summoned you today."

Vander had a fair notion but wasn't about to admit as much. "You'll have to enlighten me."

Giving a pinched frown, his father opened the file folder. He withdrew a single page of newsprint, turned it to face Vander, and slid it across the desk. "Care to explain this?"

Vander peered at the gossip column:

. . .

The Rake Review
By The Brazen Belle

May 1, 1820

Dearest reader,
    Rough winds may shake the darling buds of May, whose blooms, many a poet has observed, are all too fleeting.
    Not so the rakes of London, who are boundless in their multitudes. This month, as always, your diligent Belle has sifted through this interminable supply, and found a rake who has risen above his fellows:
    Mr. E— B—
    It is fortunate that the posterior view of Mr. E—B— is so exceptionally fine because that is the vantage point from which a woman is most likely to see him: walking away. Why, in the last six months, he has taken up and promptly discarded eight different lovers, and not the sort of women who are accustomed to being cast aside. It seems that even London's most sought-after courtesans are incapable of holding his interest for more than a fortnight. Perhaps it came as some consolation that, as the scion of one of the wealthiest families in England, he has left some truly spectacular parting gifts in his wake. Although the opera singer your faithful columnist was able to interview was disconsolate to have had the pleasure of Mr. E—B—'s company for only one night, the pleasure of his company in this case not being a mere platitude.
    Although he is the worst kind of scoundrel, Mr. E—B— is not without his virtues. During his latest turn in the boxing ring, no fewer than six ladies swooned, but not due to the bloody and violent

3

nature of the sport. No, they were overcome in the moment Mr. E—
B— removed his shirt. Thanks to the successful shipping insurance
company founded by his father, he is absurdly wealthy. And Mr. E
—B— apparently inherited his father's considerable mathematical
acumen, as my investigation revealed that he achieved the rank of
third wrangler while at Cambridge! Why this accomplishment is
not better known remains a mystery.

Still, the man is more slippery than an eel rubbed with lard,
and for all his brains, has the attention span of a gnat. Given his
inability to apply himself to anything for more than a fortnight, he
seems likely to run his father's business into the ground. And, given
the number of lovers he has taken in the last year alone, one trembles
to think how many varieties of the pox he might be harboring at the
tender age of eight and twenty.

In short, should you see Mr. E—B— around town, I must
advise you to take this notorious rakehell as your model and walk
away. Although I know the ladies of London will not heed my
warning. How is it possible that every rake I have featured thus far
has found himself caught in the parson's mousetrap? Will Mr. E—
B— suffer the same fate?

I suppose we will soon find out. Until next month, I remain
Brazenly Yours,
The Belle

When Vander looked up, his father's cheeks had gone ruddy. "Did
you know about this?"

Of course, Vander had known about it. Ever since the first
Rake Review column appeared in January, it was all anyone could
talk about. Given Vander's reputation for being a scoundrel
amongst scoundrels, his friends had placed bets back in January
about which month Vander would be featured.

Charlie Dingwell had been the one to put his hundred

pounds on May. Vander was going to make Charlie stand him a drink. It seemed like the least he could do.

Still, Vander wasn't about to admit culpability to his father. The columnist's use of initials offered him a sliver of plausible deniability.

He made sure his face was very neutral as he replied, "Of course. Everyone reads the *Rake Review*. What about it?"

His father leaned forward, narrowing his eyes. "And does this month's subject not feel slightly... familiar?"

Vander shrugged. "I don't believe it's anyone in my circle of friends."

"Do you take me for a fool, Evander?" his father snapped. "How many twenty-eight-year-old third wranglers with the initials E.B. could there possibly be?"

Shit. His father likely had him there. Still, he wasn't quite ready to admit defeat.

Vander made his eyes wide, and, he hoped, innocent. "Surely you're not suggesting that *I* am the subject?"

His father jerked open one of his desk drawers. "I cannot tell you how fervently I prayed there might be someone else to whom it could refer." He pulled a booklet from the drawer and slapped it down on the desk.

Vander peered at the title. *The Cambridge University Calendar.* He wondered if his father had gone out and purchased the latest edition, or if he subscribed to it every year for the pleasure of turning to the list of award winners from the year 1783 and seeing the words *Senior Wrangler* next to his own name, signifying that he had been the top student in mathematics from all of Cambridge's colleges in the year he took his degree.

His father jabbed a finger against the booklet. "But I have checked the list, and there is only one third wrangler with the initials E.B. You!" He glared daggers at Vander from behind his spectacles. "This is awful!"

"It really is," Vander said, dropping his pretense of innocence.

"This Brazen Belle woman said I have the pox. I don't have the pox! I *always use a sheath*."

His father pinched the bridge of his nose. "A cold comfort, at best, when now the whole world knows my son has slept with *eight women* in the past six months."

Vander brushed this off with a flick of his wrist. "Eight women. That sounds"—*about right*, his brain supplied, but he obviously couldn't say that, so he went with—"exaggerated. Who are these eight women, I should like to know?"

His father pulled a handwritten list from that irritating file folder of his. "According to the private investigator I hired to confirm whether or not the lurid details in this column were factual, they include the widow Mary Louise Huntley, the actress Marguerite Cadieux..."

Vander's attention drifted as his father listed off the names. How like his father to have hired a private investigator to make sure he had the upper hand. Who cared how many women Vander had slept with? Society didn't even blink if married men kept mistresses, much less a young, unencumbered man such as himself.

"... and Eliza Mernock, who is"—his father paused, squinting at the list as if he could not believe his eyes—"a contortionist."

"They included Eliza on there?" Vander said, outraged. "That's just low. I scarcely even slept with her."

His father placed the list back in the folder, then slapped the cover closed. "I hope you appreciate what a disaster this is!"

"Oh, I do. In addition to claiming I had the pox, that Brazen Belle woman had the gall to print that I was third wrangler!"

His father stiffened. "And what, I should like to know, is wrong with that?"

Vander rolled his eyes. He should never have acquiesced to his father's demand that he sit for the Tripos exam during his final year at Cambridge. Vander was always so, so careful to maintain his image as a devil-may-care Corinthian. Attending lectures was the least fashionable thing one could do at university, and so he hadn't done it, not even once.

But the truth was... he did find mathematics interesting, so in his spare time, he had read the various mathematical texts assigned by his tutors. And the one and only thing he had in common with his father was a brain that absorbed mathematics like a sponge.

Everyone had been shocked when Vander, described by his tutor as a "non-reading" man, had posted the best result on the written portion of the Tripos exam. There were whispered accusations that he must have cheated. The problem was that he was the only one to have successfully solved most of the differential equations. Exactly whom was he supposed to have copied? When someone pointed out who his father was, the heads of house shrugged and placed Vander in the top group for the final portion of the exam, which consisted of a debate in Latin.

Because Vander had never applied himself in Latin, he had performed atrociously in the debate, finishing third out of his three-man group, much to his father's chagrin. To Vander, however, the real tragedy had been the dent this so-called "honor" had put in his reputation.

"What's wrong with it?" Vander huffed. "Do you know what Joseph Pickering called me yesterday? A *quiz*."

His father, who had probably been called a quiz every single day during his school years, and who no doubt considered it the highest possible compliment, stared at him blankly. "And this is a problem because..."

"I called him out," Vander snapped. "And I made it very clear that anyone who repeated the remark would have to face me, either at dawn or in the ring."

His father pinched the bridge of his nose. "That is another thing we need to discuss. I cannot fathom, Evander, why you would risk your mental acuity by getting bashed in the head in the name of 'sport.'"

"I don't get bashed in the head." Vander ducked his chin and threw a few swift punches. "The best defense is a good offense. I get my opponent on his heels right from the bell and end the match in a matter of minutes. It's my signature."

His father's face was a portrait of skepticism. "So, you're saying that you never get hit in the head?"

"Hardly ever," Vander grumbled. He spun the ledger of figures he'd been correcting around to face his father and pushed it across the desk. "You seem awfully concerned about my waning mental capacity. It seems you should look to yourself."

His father winced, processing the columns in a single glance. "This is... atrocious," he agreed. "But I didn't do these figures."

"Who did?" Vander asked, surprised. His father had a strong aversion to delegating tasks. To be sure, running an insurance company, he had a dozen accountants on his payroll. But these, the overall numbers for the corporation, he trusted to no one but himself.

It was one of the reasons his father worked fourteen-hour days. Vander couldn't imagine how he did it. Fourteen hours of drudgery, locked in the dim little closet of an office he kept at the company's headquarters, every day for the rest of his life?

He would much prefer to get bashed in the head.

"I thought I would let Milton have a try at the account books," his father explained. "I see now that he was... not ready."

Vander grunted. Milton, who was Vander's first cousin on his father's side, was one year younger than Vander at twenty-seven. If Milton couldn't do basic bookkeeping by now, it didn't seem likely that he was ever going to improve, but it felt uncharitable to say as much.

Vander and Milton could not be more different in terms of temperament. They'd attended school together, and Milton wasn't a bad sort of chap. But whereas Vander had made a name for himself pulling legendary pranks with his best friend, David, Milton was a dyed-in-the-wool rule follower.

Milton probably would have been thrilled if someone had

called him a quiz, but alas, the famous Beauclerk brains had passed him over. Vander couldn't help but feel a twinge of guilt that he had been the one to get them when he had so little use for them.

And, unlike Vander, Milton absolutely adored his father's insurance business, Beauclerk Marine Casualty, and had applied to work there as soon as he completed his education.

His father narrowed his eyes at Vander. "Returning to the matter at hand—this column is a disaster!"

Vander rolled his eyes. "It'll blow over. Come June there will be a new rake-of-the-month for people to titter over. Everyone will be talking about whether *he* will get caught in the parson's mousetrap, as the first four rakes did, and I will be forgotten."

There was something steely in his father's gaze that Vander didn't care for. "As the first *five* rakes did, you mean."

Vander snorted. "Not like the first five. I'm number five, remember? And I have no intention of being caught."

His father's nostrils flared as if this short, mousy man was going to breathe fire. "Oh, yes, you do. You are going to start leading a respectable life, and that includes marrying a respectable woman, and you are going to do it before month's end." His father leaned forward over the desk, eyes boring into Vander's. "Or I am going to leave Beauclerk Marine Casualty to your cousin Milton."

Chapter Two

Vander blinked at his father, waiting for him to burst into his signature nasal chuckle, the one he used whenever someone suggested he do something completely ridiculous, like employ the Woodhousian Method of Graduation with regard to mortality tables.

It took him a good ten seconds to realize that his father wasn't joking.

Vander found he had risen halfway out of his seat. He forced himself to settle back down. "Don't... Don't be absurd! You can't leave the company to *Milton!*"

"I can, and I will!"

"Did we not just establish that Milton cannot *add*?" Vander raked a hand through his raven-black hair. "How in seven hells is he supposed to run an insurance company?"

"At least Milton will show up!" his father shot back. "Believe me, I would rather leave it to you. You're my son, and if you would but apply yourself, you are more than capable of running this company." He stood, placing both hands on the desk and leaning forward. "But right now, not only are you failing to apply yourself, you are actively driving Beauclerk Marine Casualty toward bankruptcy!"

Vander gave his father a sour look. "First you accuse me of failing to show up—which is fair. Then in your next breath, you say I'm somehow driving the company toward bankruptcy. Which is it, Father?"

His father's voice shook with feeling. "If you think it is a trivial matter that all the world now knows that the man who will one day take over Beauclerk Marine Casualty is a dissolute wastrel, then you are very much mistaken."

Vander shrugged a negligent shoulder. "I'm not the head of Beauclerk Marine Casualty. So long as you're here, business will be fine."

"Balderdash!" his father cried, slapping both hands down upon the desk. "Business is not fine! Every day since this confounded column came out, I have had clients come into my office, seeking reassurance that Beauclerk Marine Casualty is not in danger. We sell insurance, and the entire point of insurance is that it must be steady. When our clients are having a disaster, we must be there for them, as solid as a rock. Our clients do not buy a policy that lasts for one day; they buy one that lasts for the entire length of their ship's voyage. If our clients believe that the business will founder the second you take over, the question that follows is whether Beauclerk Marine Casualty will be able to honor its financial obligations."

It was a fair argument, and Vander didn't have a ready retort. "Well... it's a moot point because you're in excellent health. You'll be around for another forty years."

"Life is uncertain, Evander, which anyone purchasing insurance understands all too well." His father began to pace the room. "As insurers, our duty to our clients is a *sacred* one. After all, who is it that we turn to on the worst days of our lives?" He spun around, raising a finger for emphasis. "To our insurers!"

"*Oh, my God,*" Vander muttered, sinking down in his chair.

He recognized the opening lines of his father's speech about the virtues of insurance.

He knew from experience that the torture would last for at least ten minutes. Settling back in his chair, he allowed his thoughts to drift.

When he blinked out of his stupor some minutes later, he saw that his father had whipped himself into a frenzy. "What is the balm that greases the skids of the economy? Insurance! What allows us to rest easy as we lay on our pillows at night? Insurance! Why is it that men dare to cross oceans?" He spun around, shaking his fist at the ceiling. "Because they have insurance!"

Vander cleared his throat. "Yes, yes. Insurance. The root of every virtue. But what does this have to do with me?"

His father sank into the plain wooden chair behind his desk. "Because of the exceptionally cold winter, the sailing season to India is just getting underway. A disproportionate number of ship owners are therefore looking for insurers to underwrite their voyages right now. They will either choose Beauclerk Marine Casualty, as many of them have in years past, or they will take their business elsewhere. It is therefore imperative that we take immediate steps to demonstrate the stability of the company. There are two possible ways we can do this. The first involves you marrying a respectable woman and abandoning your life of carnality and vice."

The anger abruptly went out of his father. His shoulders sagged, and his eyes looked tired. "And the second option involves me publicly stating that you will have nothing to do with the running of Beauclerk Marine Casualty, now, or in the future."

Vander sighed. He knew full well he had always been a disappointment to his father. He may have inherited his father's brains, but at heart, he was like his mother, the adventuresome spirit who had agreed to marry a man she had known for all of three weeks and cross an ocean, leaving behind her family, her homeland of India, and the only life she had ever known.

"No more scandals," his father continued. "You will marry a respectable woman by month's end. And you will begin coming into the offices so you can learn the business. Those are my terms."

Vander rose. "And I will consider them."

His father squinted at him. "Consider them? What do you mean, consider them? What choice do you have?"

Vander was already striding out the door. "You'll see."

Once he was alone in the hallway, he allowed himself to slump against the wall. If he was being honest with himself, his life had been going to hell in a handbasket even prior to his father's pronouncement.

And it was all the fault of his best friend, David.

David Daughtry was better known by his courtesy title, Viscount Trundley, as he was heir to the Earl of Baldridge. He and Vander had been inseparable from the moment they met at Eton. In David, Vander had found a true kindred spirit, someone who believed that life should be a lark and didn't take things too seriously. For the past sixteen years, David had been the companion Vander preferred above all others, and the feeling had been mutual.

Until last month.

Her name was Miss Emily Arbuthnot, and she was the particular friend of David's little sister, Letty. Emily Arbuthnot had blue eyes and a mass of curly blonde hair. She was of middling height and average figure, and she cloaked that average figure in the shroud of muslin favored by respectable unmarried misses. Her interests, from what Vander could tell, primarily consisted of reading lurid novels. The few times Vander had encountered her, she had spent most of their conversation speaking with great enthusiasm about whatever far-fetched Gothic tale she had just finished.

She was not, in summary, the type of woman David and Vander liked. They liked sophisticated women. Seductive women.

Women clad in crimson silk, not pale pink muslin. Women who whispered wicked suggestions in your ear, not prim, virginal misses who bored you by recounting the entire plot of *The Sepulchral Summons*, whatever the hell that was.

And yet... David *liked* her! He liked her so well that, as utterly incomprehensible as it seemed to Vander, he had gone and *proposed*.

Now all David could talk about was Emily this and Emily that, and that was on the increasingly rare occasions Vander even got to see him. Half the time Vander suggested they go to Gentleman Jackson's to box a few rounds, David already had plans to call upon Emily or to take her to The Temple of the Muses, the largest bookshop in London.

And what was worse, suddenly all of their usual haunts were deemed unseemly for a man about to be married. Houses of ill repute were completely out of the question. If they so much as went to the theater, David wanted to sit next to Emily in her parents' box, not down in the pit where courtesans prowled, looking for a new protector, and there was the potential for something interesting to happen.

David refused to even cross the threshold of their favorite gaming hell as there were "too many loose women" roaming about—which had previously been at least half the point.

Vander had confronted David. If they couldn't go to any of their usual spots, when was he supposed to see him?

David had proceeded to shock him by confessing that for him, their old haunts had been growing stale for some time. "We must've gone to Boodle's to gamble and get drunk a hundred times."

This was, of course, incorrect. During the Season, they had been going around twice a week for the past six years, which would make their number of visits closer to three hundred.

Vander didn't say this aloud, of course. That was the sort of thing a *quiz* would say.

"The first few times we went, it was exciting," David had continued. "But now, on the hundredth visit? It just feels dull. Do you mean to tell me you're not tired of it, too?"

David did have a point. Vander couldn't deny that their usual antics were no longer as exciting as they once had been.

But David was approaching this problem from entirely the wrong direction. The answer wasn't to marry and settle down. It was to find even more dissolute entertainments, and even more daring women to take as their lovers.

Hence Vander's quest in the last six months to find a woman who could hold his interest. It had not proved to be Mary Louise Huntley, Marguerite Cadieux, Eliza Mernock, or any of the others.

But she was out there. He felt sure of it.

But David didn't see it that way. The man was actually excited about marrying Emily and starting a family! He had been spending more time with his father, discussing the workings of the estate he would one day inherit, and he had recently decided to run for a seat in the House of Commons.

He had even begun reading the *Farmer's Magazine*. Vander didn't know who his best friend was anymore.

He had already been feeling adrift, and now his father sprang this nonsense about marrying on him. Well, Vander wasn't ready to throw in the towel just yet. It was possible that he would have no choice but to capitulate to his father's demands, so logic dictated that he start looking for a suitable bride, just in case.

But if he could find a way to support himself, he could thumb his nose at his father and continue living as he damn well pleased.

Sighing, Vander made his way downstairs. He nodded grimly to the butler as he accepted his hat and gloves when a voice interrupted his whirling thoughts. "Vander? Is that you, *azizam*?"

He looked up. "*Maman*."

His mother was descending the stairs. The passage of thirty years may have left faint creases at the corners of her eyes and a

15

trace of grey in her dark mane, but it had not dimmed the beauty that had caused his square, prudent-to-a-fault father to take one look at the woman who now bore the name Azita Beauclerk and fall head-over-heels in love.

His father had sailed for India to better understand the voyage many of the ships covered by his budding insurance company would undertake. He had planned to come back with information that would help him make better underwriting decisions.

Instead, he had returned with a bride.

It was his mother Vander took after, and thank God for that. Far better to have her copper skin, fine dark eyes, thick raven waves, and graceful bearing than his father's short stature, beady grey eyes, thinning hair, and ashen complexion. Although... to be fair, his father wouldn't be half so pallid if he ever set foot outside his office.

But it wasn't merely in terms of looks that Vander resembled his mother; he had inherited her spirit as well. When his father had begged her to leave her country, her family, and everything she had ever known behind and cross the ocean with him on the strength of three weeks' acquaintance, this was the woman who had laughed and replied, "Why not?"

Vander couldn't fathom why his mother had said yes. He could understand her yearning for adventure well enough. But how on earth had this free-spirited woman looked at his *father*, whose idea of a wild night was putting two sugars in his tea, and thought, *now there is my life partner?*

His mother had laughed when he asked her about it. "I had your father marked from the start. I did long to see the world, but my *maman* always told me, 'Azita, the most important thing is to find a man who will treat you like a queen.' And I knew at once that was Cedric." She smiled triumphantly. "I was right."

Reaching the bottom of the stairs, his mother framed his face. "You look as if your spirits are low. I take it you spoke with your father?"

As always, they spoke in Persian, the official court language of Hyderabad, where his mother had grown up, liberally sprinkled with whatever English terms lacked a precise equivalent. "*Maman*, he says I have to marry."

She laughed, a bright, sparkling sound. "Look at your face—you would think marriage was a medieval form of torture."

Vander flicked an eyebrow toward the ceiling. "Is it not?"

She shook her head, but she was smiling. "There is an age for everything. You are not two and twenty anymore. It will be all right. You will see." She took his hands in hers and pressed them, looking him in the eye. "Vander... ask Letty."

Vander blinked at her. "Letty? You mean... David's little sister?"

"Of course."

It hadn't occurred to him that he could ask Letty for help. But now that he thought on it... it was the perfect solution.

Lady Leticia Daughtry was about the only respectable young lady he knew, after all. She was bound to know the other debutantes, to know which ones were all right and which ones were prone to hysterics.

Letty would be the perfect person to advise him. She could even introduce him to some likely girls, and if Vander's other plans fell through and he had no choice but to marry, at least he would wind up with a bride who was relatively tolerable.

Vander smiled for the first time all morning. "Why didn't I think of that? That's just what I'll do—I'll ask Letty."

"Good!" His mother beamed at him.

"I'm even dining at Daughtry House tonight," Vander added. A formal dinner was an event he normally would have avoided. But David had been nagging him to dine with his family for the past week, and considering such stuffy occasions were his only opportunities to see his best friend these days, he had grudgingly agreed to attend.

"Perfect! You will stop here afterward and let me know what she says, won't you?"

"Hmm?" He wasn't sure there would be much to report. He would ask Letty to choose a few young ladies for him to meet, and she would say yes. The more interesting part would be when she actually started making introductions. But his mother's eyes were imploring, so he bowed. "Of course, *Maman*."

His mother clasped her hands. "Oh, I will be waiting with bated breath! Cedric," she called to his father, who had appeared at the top of the stairs, "come quickly. I have the best news!"

Once he reached the bottom of the stairs, his father bowed over his mother's hand, pressing a lingering kiss against her knuckles. "What is it, my queen?"

"Vander is going to ask Letty!"

His father swung around to face Vander. "That is good news, indeed!" He reached out and squeezed Vander's upper arm. "Well done, son."

"Right." Vander wasn't sure why they were making such a fuss over his asking Letty to advise him. But if it got them off his back for the next few weeks, he wasn't about to complain. "Well, then. I think I'll head over to Gentleman Jackson's and go a few rounds."

"Yes, yes," his mother said, shooing him out the door. "Go and have your fun, but do not forget your promise to come back tonight and tell me everything!"

Vander would do that. He would go and box. That would clear his mind.

Because he had some planning to do if he was going to figure out how to avoid his father's trap.

Chapter Three

Letty had known Vander was going to be in attendance at the dinner her mother was hosting.

Her mother had mentioned it over breakfast three days ago, which meant she had spent the past three days feeling nervous and fluttery.

These days, when she saw him at all, it was invariably in passing. When he and David had been at school together, he would often come and stay with them during school holidays.

But for the past few years, he and David had preferred to go out, usually late at night, and to places Letty was not permitted to know about.

David had changed his habits since he began courting Emily. Now Letty saw her brother all the time.

But Vander remained elusive.

And so, she had spent the past three days trying to temper her expectations. Just because Vander was coming here did not mean she would speak with him, and if she did, it would probably be nothing more than a short greeting. He was here to see David, not her.

Besides, there was no possibility of her being seated next to him at dinner. Once, when she was sixteen, she had asked her mother if she could sit next to Vander.

Her mother had laughed. "Oh, Letty—let me save you some heartache, dear. Put thoughts of Evander Beauclerk out of your mind. You are not for the likes of him, darling."

So, there was the fact that her own mother thought she stood no chance with a man so rakish and dashing. But even if he wasn't such an obvious catch, Vander was as droll as he was handsome, the life of every party. *Everyone* wanted to sit next to Vander.

Letty, on the other hand? She was *nice*. Which sounded good in theory, but in practice, nice girls were assigned to sit next to the most disagreeable person at the party, because they were too polite to complain about it. If Letty had a shilling for every time a hostess had beamed as she informed her that she would be sitting next to the Dowager Countess of Accrington, who would spend all evening railing against "young people these days," or Herbert Twisleton-Ford-Trefusis, who would complain incessantly about his gout, she could buy herself a Kashmiri shawl.

"It's such a relief to have you here, Letty," the hostess would say, pressing her hand. And someone else—the diamond of the Season, or an alluring young widow, would wind up seated next to the handsome young earl or the poet known for being a great wit because they would complain bitterly and spread vile gossip about the hostess if she dared to seat them next to a dreadful bore.

Letty didn't want to be *nice* anymore. Although... that wasn't quite right. Of course she wanted to be nice!

She just didn't want to be taken advantage of. She wanted to have *fun* at parties, not be assigned to dance attendance upon the most boring person in the room. She wanted to drink champagne, to laugh, to try her hand at being a great wit. Because she thought she could, given half a chance. She wasn't a debutante, fresh out of the schoolroom, anymore. She was three and twenty, she was well-read, and she didn't have a missish bone in her body.

Not that anyone noticed, especially Vander, who seemed to think she was still ten years old.

Letty sighed. Even though she knew she was unlikely to spend any significant time in Vander's company, she had dressed carefully. She wore a white gown with a sash in her favorite color, purple, in a shade that perfectly matched the wisteria flowers embroidered about the neckline and hem.

Now, she was standing in the crimson parlor, chatting with her friend Emily and trying to feign ignorance of the fact that the man she had spent the last thirteen years pining after was somewhere in the room when someone seized her elbow.

She knew it was him without turning her head. If someone had blindfolded her and taken her to the Scarborough Fair, she could've picked Vander out of the crowd by his cinnamon-and-ginger shaving tonic. In an instant, her heart was flying.

He leaned down and she felt his breath on her ear as he murmured, "I need to speak with you." Now her whole body was atremble.

At last, she turned to look at him. "Vander." She pressed a hand to her heart and laughed, trying to brush off the breathless quality of her voice. "You startled me."

His eyes were dark brown with flecks of bronze in them. Letty had always found that once she looked into them, it was curiously difficult to tear her eyes away.

Vander did not seem to suffer from the same difficulty, because he had turned to Emily. "You don't mind if I steal Letty away, do you, Miss Arbuthnot?"

Emily's blue eyes were wide as guineas because of course, she knew about Letty's hopeless infatuation with Vander. Emily waved her fan a trifle over-enthusiastically. "Not at all! You two go right ahead. Your timing could not be more fortunate, because I was just going to visit the, um... you know, the... the..." She cleared her throat, her cheeks flushing pink. "Excuse me!"

Vander tilted his head to the side as he stared after Emily's retreating form, but then he shrugged and offered his arm to Letty. "Shall we?"

Letty placed her hand gingerly on his arm, trying to suppress the shudder that ran down her spine. "Of course."

Much to her surprise, he led her out of the crimson parlor and down the hall. The library and the portrait gallery were occupied, and so he led her farther back into the house, ushering her into her father's private study.

He shut the door behind them, and now fairies were dancing in Letty's stomach.

The room was dark, illuminated only by the fire crackling in the grate. Vander settled Letty in one of the leather wing chairs that flanked the fireplace, then lit a few candles before taking the seat opposite hers.

"Letty," he began, raking a hand through his silky black hair. This would have ruined most coiffures, but Vander's hair immediately fell back into its customary tousled perfection.

Frankly, Letty was surprised that the Brazen Belle had not mentioned Vander's hair in the portion of her column in which she extolled his best features. Letty *loved* Vander's hair and longed to run her fingers through it. Of course, not being permitted to attend something as scandalous as a boxing match, she had never seen Vander take off his shirt or even had the chance to properly appreciate *the view from behind*, as the Belle had put it, because of the prevailing fashion for tailcoats. Perhaps if she were given the chance to experience those delights, she, too, would forget all about his hair.

His eyes were imploring as he said, "There is something I wanted to ask you."

She parted her lips to ask what it was when the door to the study opened.

Vander cast a hard look toward the door. "Leave us," he said, voice as dark as midnight. Letty could just make out a servant's muffled apology and the click of the door over the thundering of her heart.

She reminded herself not to get her hopes up because this was *not* a proposal. She had a rare talent for taking completely ordinary gestures from Vander and spinning them into something romantic, such as the time when she was fourteen and he had asked her to pass the salt. By the time dinner was over, she had managed to invent a whole story interpreting the brush of his thumb against hers as a sign of unrequited longing, even though he had not so much as looked at her for the rest of the meal.

She cleared her throat. "What did you want to speak to me about?"

"I need to ask you for a terrible favor. I'm sure you saw that I was featured in the *Rake Review*."

Letty felt her cheeks flush. It was, of course, all anyone could talk about. And thanks to the Brazen Belle, Letty now knew all kinds of scandalous details about Vander, many of which she would have preferred not to know.

She cleared her throat. "Yes, I saw the column."

He paused, a muscle working in his jaw. "My father is demanding that I marry."

Now Letty's heart was stampeding like a cavalry charge. "Oh?" she whispered.

He made an elegant gesture with his wrist. "And I was trying to think *who* I could possibly marry." His brown eyes, throwing off sparks from the firelight, bore into hers. "And then, I thought of you."

Oh God oh God oh God, this was actually happening! Perhaps it shouldn't come entirely as a surprise. Three weeks ago, Letty, who had previously been regarded as something of a wallflower, had received not one, but two proposals—in the middle of the Sunderland ball, no less. Her mother had declared that Letty would announce which of her suitors she would marry one month hence. She now had only one week to make her decision.

The knowledge that everyone's favorite contingency plan would soon be removed from the Marriage Mart had caused the men of London to come crawling out of the woodwork. She had received six additional proposals since the Sunderland ball, all of which Letty had declined. None of those men stirred tender feelings in her, and pragmatically, their offers were not as good as those of her first two suitors—Lord Throckmorton, who was a baron with a reasonably large estate, and Bertie Strickleton, who was due to inherit the fortune of a childless aunt and uncle.

But the point was, those public proposals had caused men to consider her afresh.

As Vander was doing now.

Letty swallowed thickly. "You thought of me? Truly?"

"I did." He chuckled. "You were actually my mother's suggestion. But as soon as she said your name..." He paused, waving a hand as he searched for the words. "It felt... right."

Oh, this was better than she could have hoped! To be sure, Vander was proposing a pragmatic arrangement. His father was forcing him to wed, he had said. He did not harbor for her the sorts of tender feelings she had long felt for him.

But that was all right. Letty knew that they were meant to be together. All she needed was a chance. He would come to see how compatible they were. She was certain of it.

And now, she would get that chance.

"Yes." She laughed at her own trembling voice, swiping a thumb beneath her eyes. "Of course, the answer is yes, Vander."

"Good." He nodded. "Good. It's such a relief, knowing that you'll help me out of this predicament."

Letty smiled, not quite trusting herself to speak. Of course, that was all he thought she was doing. Little did he know that this was not a favor she was granting him, but her own heart's desire.

There was no need to tell him that today. She would confess her feelings once he had come to realize his own.

"So." Vander leaned forward, placing his elbows upon his

knees. "Is there anybody you have in mind? With whom you think I might suit?"

It took a moment for the words to penetrate Letty's fog of happiness. Even then, she was certain she must have misheard. "I'm sorry... What do you mean, someone with whom you might *suit*?"

"You know, some friend to whom you can introduce me, or..." Suddenly his spine went ramrod straight. Horror dawned in his eyes. "Wait... you didn't think I was proposing to *you*, did you?"

Letty gave a shrill laugh that sounded more like a pair of weasels locked in combat than a human enjoying a spot of humor. "Of course not!" she shrieked, which was, of course, a lie. But surely the Almighty would forgive her for trying to cling to one single, solitary sliver of dignity.

Vander was frowning. "Because, now that I think about it, the way I phrased that, it definitely sounded like I was—"

It was unladylike to interrupt, but Letty was not about to let him finish that sentence. "How fortunate it is that we understand each other so well, and I comprehended your meaning immediately!"

He sagged back in his chair. "That's such a relief. I mean, you're David's little sister. I would *never*—"

"Of course, you wouldn't! What an *absurd* notion!" Letty said loudly because she didn't particularly want to hear the rest of *that* sentence, either. "But you have absolutely nothing to worry about."

"Good." Vander smiled at her, then raked a hand through his perfectly tousled raven waves, and Letty's heart squeezed, he looked so absurdly handsome. "So, to whom will you introduce me?"

Letty had absolutely no idea. She had never given any thought to whom the man she adored should marry other than her. And right now, the crushing disappointment of having had her most impossible dream granted and then dashed in an instant left her incapable of coherent thought. "Give me some time to consider it."

Vander nodded. "Very well."

She cleared her throat. "Lady Cumberland is hosting a garden party tomorrow. Will you be in attendance?"

"She's friends with my mother, so I imagine we will have received an invitation."

"Perfect. I will give the matter some thought and endeavor to introduce you to someone at the garden party." Letty paused, peering at him. "Are there any particular qualities you require in your future bride?"

Vander looked befuddled. "Qualities? I haven't given it the slightest thought." He paused, staring into the fire. "I'll want someone who is extremely beautiful, obviously."

"Obviously." Someone extremely beautiful. *Unlike you, Letty.* She dug her nails into the palm of her hand, hoping the shock of pain would stop the tears that were suddenly welling in her eyes. "All right, then," she said with forced brightness. "Let me see what I can do."

Vander rose and offered his arm. "We should be getting back. I'm sure dinner will begin shortly."

"I'm sure you're right." Letty looped her arm through his, forced a smile to her lips, and prepared to endure the longest dinner in the history of the world.

Chapter Four

After dining with David's family, Vander stopped by his parents' townhouse. He was surprised to find his mother pacing the foyer.

Her slippers clicked against the marble tiles as she hurried to him. "Did you ask her? What did she say?"

Vander paused in the act of handing his hat and gloves to a footman. "She said yes, of course."

His mother clapped her hands, looking disproportionately excited for such a trivial piece of news. "*Of course*. Listen to you, so sure of yourself. But this is wonderful news! I must call on Lady Baldridge tomorrow. We have a wedding to plan!"

Vander quirked his head to the side. "Shouldn't that wait until I've actually selected my bride?"

His mother's expression darkened in an instant. "What do you mean, until you've selected your bride? You asked Letty, did you not?"

"I asked her to help me find a bride, yes."

"You asked her to..." His mother gave a cry of frustration as she whirled away, her hands curling into claws. "How is this possible? I married your father, the mathematical genius, specifically so I would not find myself with a child who is as dumb as a donkey!"

Vander flinched. "Maman? Why would you say that?"

She pointed a finger at him. "I told you to ask Letty!"

It almost sounded as if his mother had thought he was going to propose to Letty. But that couldn't possibly be right. To be sure, for a second there, he had thought Letty had misinterpreted his question. But she hadn't, and she had agreed that the mere notion was absurd.

So, he nodded slowly. "And I did."

His mother crossed the room in three quick strides. "I meant to ask Letty to marry you!" she hissed. "Not to help you find some other bride!"

"*Marry Letty?*" Vander shut his jaw, which had fallen slack. "I can't marry Letty!"

"I should like to know why not!"

Because she is ten years old, his brain supplied, although he knew that was wrong. He settled on, "She's too young."

His mother crossed her arms. "She is three and twenty."

He had to admit, that did sound like a fairly reasonable age to marry. But still, he couldn't marry *Letty*. "Maman, I can't marry Letty. She deserves someone who will treat her like a queen."

His mother's voice was dangerous as she replied, "And you do not plan to treat your wife like a queen?"

Clearly *that* had been the wrong thing to say. Vander struggled to regroup. "But she's David's little sister! David would kill me if I dishonored her."

His mother threw her hands up. "I did not suggest that you dishonor her. I said for you to marry her! What could be more honorable than that?"

Vander shook his head. "David is one of the most important people in my life. He's the nearest thing I have to a brother. I won't do anything to jeopardize my friendship with him."

"You would be strengthening your friendship, not jeopardizing it. If you marry his sister, you would be his brother in truth. How is that not a good thing?"

Vander's jaw clenched. His mother didn't understand. David had watched him cut a swath through half the courtesans in London. It was one thing to go carousing with the man who had once won a two-hundred-pound bet by fucking all three Milthorpe triplets, Polly, Molly, and Dolly, in the space of half an hour.

But one would not permit such a man to go within a thousand yards of his little sister.

"Out of the question," Vander said.

His mother made a sound of exasperation. "Who will you find who suits you as well as Letty? No one, that's who. But why should you listen to me? What would I know about a happy marriage?" She shook her head. "It was not like this in my day. Never did I question my elders. Never!"

The lecture that ensued was almost as familiar as his father's speech on the sacred importance of insurance, so Vander listened with just half an ear, muttering apologies and reassurances in all the requisite places, then made his escape as quickly as he could.

Striding out into the night, Vander headed not toward his bachelor apartments, but toward St. James's Street.

It was time to see if the plan he had spent the better part of the afternoon formulating had any chance of working. If he was right, if he could make this hair-brained scheme work, maybe he wouldn't need Letty's help finding a bride after all.

Chapter Five

For someone who had spent most of the previous evening sobbing into her pillow, Letty thought she looked remarkably fresh as she caught a glimpse of herself in the mirror that hung in Lady Cumberland's foyer.

It was the pink gown she had chosen. It flattered her creamy complexion and brightened her plain brown hair and eyes. She had mostly chosen it because she knew her mother would chastise her if she wore purple to two events in a row. Purple, her mother maintained, was for royalty and women with the sophistication to pull the color off.

Letty sighed. Apparently, she wasn't even interesting enough to wear her favorite color.

But the pink was proving to be an inspired choice. She was feeling almost pretty until she stepped into the back garden and beheld the woman to whom she had resolved to introduce Vander.

Vander wanted someone beautiful? Well, Priscilla Peabody was considered to be the diamond of the Season. She had blonde hair. Blue eyes. Rose lips. A figure that was the perfect blend of slender and curvaceous.

And what was even better, she was the daughter of a baron who had run up significant debts expanding his horse racing operation. Letty felt certain that any woman with a pulse would be thrilled by the prospect of being Vander's bride. But some noble families might turn their noses up at him because his father was *in trade*.

Not Priscilla Peabody's family. Vander's father was one of the richest men in London. He was exactly the sort of man Lord Peabody needed his daughter to catch.

Letty forced a smile to her lips as she approached Priscilla. As easy as it was to be jealous of a girl who had received such natural gifts, Priscilla had never been anything but kind to her. And, in a way, their situations were much the same. Letty had to choose amongst her small handful of suitors, and Priscilla had to choose a man with a fortune.

It was just that Priscilla was about to be presented with the choice Letty yearned for.

"Miss Peabody, might I ask you a question?" Letty inquired.

"Of course, Lady Leticia," Priscilla replied, smiling.

Letty dropped her voice low. "Do you have a partner for the pall-mall match? I ask because there is a particular gentleman who is in need of one. I am already paired with Lord Throckmorton, but I believe he is someone whom you might like to meet."

"Oh?" Miss Peabody smiled, but she was peering over Letty's shoulder to see who else was arriving. "Who is he?"

"Mr. Evander Beauclerk."

Miss Peabody's eyes snapped to Letty. "Evander Beauclerk!" She leaned forward and whispered, "Is he truly coming? I've been trying to make Mr. Beauclerk's acquaintance for months, but he does not usually attend events such as these."

Letty's smile felt brittle as she nodded. "I have it on good authority that he will be here. May I inform him that you will be his partner?"

Miss Peabody's laugh was slightly wild as if she could not

believe Letty even had to ask. "Please do. You may tell him I should be *delighted*." She leaned forward, placing her hand over Letty's and squeezing. "Thank you, Lady Leticia. You don't know how much this introduction means to me."

Letty blinked rapidly, as her eyes suddenly felt moist. It happened that she did appreciate what a blessing it was to spend any time in Vander's company, whether it was an afternoon or a lifetime. "You are most welcome. I'll bring him to you before the match is to commence."

"Excellent!"

Letty excused herself and crossed the garden toward the cluster of chairs where her mother was chatting with friends. As she passed by the back door, it opened, and out walked Vander.

"Good, you're here," she said, striding up to him. "I've arranged for you to partner with your first prospective bride in the pall-mall tournament."

Vander rolled his eyes theatrically. "We're playing pall-mall? Really?"

Letty glanced around to make sure no one else was within hearing distance and dropped her voice low. "If you think pall-mall is insipid, I shudder to think how you're going to get through this month."

He grunted. "It can't possibly get worse than pall-mall."

"Spoken like a man who has never been forced to play blind man's bluff with Arthur Fitzgibbon."

Vander chuckled, looking surprised. "I was at school with Fitzgibbon. I take it his habits of personal cleanliness have not improved."

"They have not, yet paradoxically, I was grateful for the stench. At least I could smell him coming." She leaned toward his ear, dropping her voice to a whisper. "Mr. Fitzgibbon does not seem to grasp the general strategy of blind man's bluff, in that the blindfolded party is the one who is supposed to do the grabbing. He is as handsy as his apparent namesake."

"Son of a gibbon," Vander said, grinning.

Letty paused, momentarily stunned by the sight of his handsome, smiling visage pointing squarely at her. "Precisely," she finally managed.

"Why do you not decline to participate, if it's so odious?"

"Would that I could. But above all else, young, unmarried ladies are expected to be *agreeable*. I am never permitted to complain about anything. In fact, I am required to express enthusiasm for all manner of horrifying things, from blind man's bluff to hair jewelry to ratafia. I therefore had to be, shall we say, creative, in dealing with Mr. Fitzgibbon."

Vander tipped his forehead toward hers. "Do tell."

"The third time his hands strayed to places they should not have been, I managed to capture him. There happened to be a young girl participating in the game, Miss Jane Burgess. She was twelve years old and very petite. So, after making a show of feeling Mr. Fitzgibbon's hands, I cheerfully declared that my captor must be Miss Burgess because only she could have such small, delicate hands."

Vander burst out laughing. "You didn't!"

Letty grinned, remembering. "I most certainly did, and wouldn't you know it, Mr. Fitzgibbon avoided me for the remainder of the game."

Vander wiped his eyes with the heel of his hand, still laughing. "I can't wrap my mind around the notion of sweet little Letty Daughtry delivering such a blistering set-down."

Letty strove to make her voice light as she replied, "Yes, well, I have grown up a bit since those summers you spent with us at Baldridge Hall."

Vander was studying her, and although it was probably a figment of her overactive imagination, Letty thought his expression was one of admiration. "You certainly have." He nodded toward the refreshment table. "So, no ratafia for you. What is your preferred libation?"

"Champagne," Letty said without hesitation. "Not that I'm permitted to have a glass at two o'clock in the... Wait, what are you doing?"

Vander had looped his arm through hers. Tugging her forward, he strode toward the back of the gardens. "Misbehaving, as usual."

Without breaking stride, he snagged two glasses of champagne from the tray of a passing footman, carrying them in one hand as he led her to the shade of a flowering crabapple tree.

Smiling, he offered one to her.

"I shouldn't." Letty peered across the garden, trying to ascertain if her mother was watching. "Mama would have a fit."

"Take it." He pressed the glass into her hand. "If anyone says something, blame me. I, of course, am entirely ignorant when it comes to these things, and you were merely too polite to point out my shocking lapse in etiquette."

"Well. When you put it that way." She sipped from her glass, unable to suppress a soft groan of pleasure.

There was just something about champagne. Maybe it was the bubbles. It made her happy.

Vander's smile was genuine. "You, Leticia Daughtry, are full of surprises."

Letty chuckled. "Have I shocked you?"

"You have, but please, continue. It is surely the only way I will survive something as tedious as pall-mall." He took a sip from his own glass. "So, who do you have in mind for me?"

Letty fought to keep any trace of sadness from crossing her features. "Miss Priscilla Peabody." She tilted her glass toward the refreshment table, where Miss Peabody stood. "She's the one in the mint-green gown. Blonde hair, blue eyes... she just accepted a glass of punch."

"I see her." Vander made an appreciative sound. "She looks promising. From this distance, anyway."

"You won't be disappointed when you see her up close. She's considered to be the diamond of this Season. I should warn you that her father has run up significant debts on his horseracing operation."

"How much?" Vander asked, his eyes not straying from Miss Peabody.

"Rumored to be in the neighborhood of thirty thousand pounds."

Vander made a dismissive sound. "That's nothing."

It was more money than most people would see in ten lifetimes and six times Letty's own dowry. Vander's father must be even more successful than everyone said if his son could shrug off such a ruinous sum.

"When I proposed you as her partner, she seemed delighted," Letty said honestly. "She does not lack for suitors, but I am under the impression that most of the men who can afford her are her father's age, or even older. She seemed excited to be meeting someone young and handsome."

"Perfect." He tore his eyes from Miss Peabody's lovely profile to look at Letty. "What about you? Who will you be playing with?"

"I will be partnering with one of my suitors. Lord Throckmorton."

Vander tilted his head. "*One* of your suitors? How many do you have?"

Letty drew herself up, unsure what he was implying. "Two."

Vander shook his head, an expression of confusion on his handsome face. "But... *suitors*. The way you phrased it sounds rather serious."

Letty rolled her eyes. Did he not believe it was possible that a man might be interested in her? "Considering they both proposed to me in the middle of Lady Sunderland's ball, I have every reason to believe their intentions are serious."

"They *what?*" Vander hissed.

Letty laughed, disbelieving. "Do you mean to tell me you have not heard of it? It has been the juiciest *on dit* for weeks." She couldn't resist poking him in the arm. "Right up until *someone* was featured in the *Rake Review.*"

Vander scowled, somehow managing to look just as handsome with a sour look on his face. "Never mind that. Who are these two suitors of yours? And what do you mean, they proposed in the middle of a ball? Surely proposing should be a private affair."

Letty took a fortifying sip of champagne. "I had promised the supper dance to Mr. Bertrand Strickleton—"

"Bertie Strickleton!" Vander looked appalled. "Tell me he's not one of the two. He's what, seventeen?"

In truth, Letty could see why Vander might be under that impression. Bertie might be slightly older in years, but he was not what you would call an old soul. But she could hardly disparage the man she very well might end up marrying, so she merely said, "He is indeed. And he is two and twenty."

Vander screwed up his nose. "And you said the other one is Throckmorton? He's what, twice your age?"

Letty tried to make her voice light. "Just fifteen years my senior."

"Good Lord. So, what happened next?"

"It turned out that Lord Throckmorton had approached my mother, and she had promised him the supper dance on my behalf. That was the source of the conflict."

Understanding flared in Vander's fine, dark eyes. "Ah, I see. I take it you didn't have any other dances free?"

Letty almost snorted but stopped herself just in time. *No other dances free.* She was a *wallflower.* She spent at least half of every ball standing in the corner with Emily.

But if Vander didn't realize that she enjoyed, at best, a middling sort of popularity, she certainly wasn't about to enlighten him. "It happens that I did have some free dances. But they were both strangely insistent upon claiming that particular one."

Vander drained his glass. "Why was that?"

"It turned out that they had both resolved to propose to me during the supper break. By the time this came out, they were shouting at each other in the middle of Lady Sunderland's ballroom. Everyone was staring. It was awful."

Vander huffed. "*Awful.* I'm pretty sure that says it all, but I'll ask, just to be sure. Do you really want to marry either of them?"

Letty felt her throat constrict. Because this was the question no one had asked her, no one save Emily. Everyone asked *which* of her suitors she was going to choose. *Whether* she preferred an older husband or a younger one.

No one had considered that she might not want either of them. Lord Throckmorton was gruff and taciturn. They'd danced together a dozen times, but he still felt like a stranger. Meanwhile, she thought of Bertie Strickleton less as a suitor, and more as a younger brother.

An *annoying* younger brother.

She blinked back the moisture suddenly welling in her eyes. "I—"

"Lady Leticia," a curt voice said.

In an instant, Letty pasted on a bright smile. "Lord Throckmorton. How lovely to see you. Are you acquainted with Mr. Evander Beauclerk?"

"Indeed. Beauclerk." Unsmiling, Lord Throckmorton extended his hand. Vander took it, but make no mistake, this handshake was not a friendly gesture. As they gripped each other's hands, the baron's face turned red, and a vein popped out on Vander's temple.

"I believe the pall-mall is about to commence," Lord Throckmorton said once the wrestling match had concluded.

"How delightful," Letty said. "Allow me to introduce Mr. Beauclerk to his partner, and we can take up our positions."

Vander pointedly scooped up Letty's hand, glowering at the baron as he placed it on his arm. Once they were a few strides away, he whispered, "I don't like this."

"It is not for you to like or dislike," Letty said firmly.

"Do you really want to marry Throckmorton?" Vander hissed, his voice tinged with disbelief.

"I don't know," Letty acknowledged. "But it would seem prudent for me to spend some time in his company so I can make an informed decision between him and Mr. Strickleton."

She glanced at Vander and found him making the expression of a man who had stepped in something exceptionally foul, likely produced by a pig. "Van-der," she chided. "Don't look so sour. Lord Throckmorton might not be the most scintillating conversationalist—"

"A rather exceptional understatement," Vander muttered.

She poked him in the arm. "But he appears to be a perfectly nice man. And it's not as if I have any other choices." Letty would never know where she got the nerve, but she found herself lifting her chin and staring him boldly in the eye. "Do I?"

The question hung in the air for six beats of Letty's pounding heart before a feminine voice said, "Lady Leticia?"

Letty forced a bright, brittle smile. "Miss Peabody, there you are. Allow me to present Mr. Evander Beauclerk. Mr. Beauclerk, Miss Priscilla Peabody."

Vander bowed neatly over Miss Peabody's hand. "Miss Peabody. A pleasure."

"The pleasure is all mine," Priscilla trilled.

Letty took a step back, considering them. In truth, they made an exceptionally attractive couple. Priscilla's glowing golden mien formed the perfect complement to Vander's dark, brooding handsomeness.

Ignoring the wave of jealousy that washed over her, Letty

cleared her throat. "I must find my own partner, so I'll leave you two to it," she said with false cheerfulness.

Vander was looking not at his lovely partner, but at her. "Wait, Letty—"

She dropped a hasty curtsy, unable to meet his eye. "Do excuse me."

Chapter Six

By the third wicket, Vander was regretting every decision he'd made in life that had led him to this point.

It wasn't that he disliked Priscilla Peabody, precisely. That would be akin to disliking... kittens, perhaps. Or syllabub. It was difficult to despise something so sweet and fluffy.

On the other hand, Vander would argue that there was a certain way one preferred to enjoy such confections.

In small doses.

"And then," Miss Peabody continued, "I said to Mama, 'What if we tried it with a *red* ribbon?'"

Vander grunted in response. Which would normally feel rude, but he had discovered in his first three minutes of Miss Peabody's acquaintance that he would not be afforded time for a more customary response, say, two entire words.

"But you will never believe this." Miss Peabody paused for emphasis, squeezing his forearm. "The red ribbon *clashed.*"

Throwing caution to the wind, Vander hazarded an entire sentence. "Is that s—"

"But *then*," Miss Peabody cried, triumphant, "it came to me! I said, 'Mama, what about this *pink* ribbon...'"

Vander wondered if it was physically possible to knock himself insensible with a pall-mall mallet in such a way that would make it look like an accident. He would be the laughingstock of London if he pulled it off.

But it might be worth it...

A few feet away, Letty appeared to be having only a slightly better time of it with Throckmorton. Vander had observed her making a number of conversational overtures, all of which withered on the vine in the face of the baron's monosyllabic answers. She had eventually given up and was now smiling across the lawn in serene silence.

What they should do was pair Miss Peabody with Throckmorton. She wouldn't notice, much less mind, that he wasn't saying a word. That would leave Vander to partner with Letty.

If he were partners with Letty, he would actually be enjoying himself. Not the pall-mall, per se. Pall-mall was still ridiculous.

But at least they could have a laugh about it. She had caught him by surprise earlier. Who would have thought that little Letty Daughtry would grow up to have such a wicked sense of humor? He had assumed—wrongly, as it turned out—that she would be prim and inane.

He was having a miserable time with Miss Peabody. But let him be partners with Letty and throw in a couple more glasses of champagne, and he would wager that the afternoon could have been, dare he say it, fun.

Beside him, Miss Peabody batted her eyes, giving no sign that she had noticed his lapsed attention. "I'll bet you cannot guess what I suggested next!"

"To try a blue ribbon?" Vander hazarded.

Her mouth fell open into a perfect little circle. "How did you know?" She shook her head as if she simply could not believe it. "You must be even more intelligent than everyone says!"

He supposed that most men would have been puffing out their chests at such a compliment. But oddly, Vander found that

41

the initial spark of attraction he had felt toward Miss Peabody had gone out.

He shrugged. "Just a lucky guess."

It was fortunate that he was in such a good mood and his stores of patience were at capacity. And if Priscilla Peabody was annoying, well, it looked like he might not have to marry her, or someone of her ilk, after all.

Last night, after dinner at David's and the conversation with his mother that had followed, he had gone to Boodle's to test out the plan that would hopefully get him out from underneath his father's thumb. Boodle's was the club where a man went when he wanted to play deep, and the site where many a fortune had been lost.

But one man's loss was another man's gain, and Vander meant to be on the winning side of that exchange. He had a few points in his favor. Thanks to the mathematical acumen he had inherited from his father, he could calculate his odds of winning any given hand with pinpoint precision. He also had a good memory for counting cards and knowing when he might press his advantage.

He hoped that, if he applied himself, he could earn a living at the gaming tables. And surely enough, last night he had walked away with a tidy profit of twenty-five pounds.

Buoyed by optimism, Vander nodded and grunted as the conversation moved on, to ribbons of yellow, green, and lilac. And he survived an afternoon of Priscilla Peabody's inane chatter.

Just barely.

Chapter Seven

After the garden party's conclusion, Letty was standing with her mother, waiting for the carriage to be brought around when Vander came striding up.

He fixed her mother with his most charming smile. "Lady Baldridge," he said, bowing over her hand. "Would it be impertinent to say how lovely you look in that shade of primrose?"

She rapped his knuckles with her fan, but she was smiling. "Not impertinent so much as obvious. What do you want, Vander?"

He looked at Letty and smiled. "Your daughter."

Letty almost swooned right onto the portico's flagstone floor. Dear God, she needed to get hold of herself. She knew full well Vander hadn't meant it like *that*.

He could not have been clearer on that point.

She tried to pretend she hadn't been attending. "Hmm? What was that, Vander?"

Her mother was looking at her strangely, but Vander said smoothly, "I was wondering if I might drive Letty home in my phaeton. It's been so long since I've seen her, and we didn't get much of a chance to talk at the party."

"Of course. So long as you convey her straight home, as we've another engagement this evening." Her mother leaned forward, giving Vander a firm look. "And you are to keep the hood open, young man."

"Thank you, my lady." Vander was already towing Letty toward his phaeton, a flashy highflyer in cherry red drawn by an exquisitely matched pair of dark bays. He helped boost her up into the seat, then climbed up beside her, taking the reins.

As the horses started forward, Letty squeezed her eyes shut. This was one of those moments she had always dreamed about, Vander taking her for a ride in his highflyer. Even though she knew he wasn't doing so out of any sort of interest in her, she knew with a dreadful certainty that she would be revisiting this moment a thousand times in her daydreams.

She shook herself. She mustn't be so obvious in her mooning. She pulled her fan from her reticule and snapped it open, attempting to look nonchalant. "So. What did you think of Miss Peabody?"

Vander steered his team into a corner. "I hope this does not come across as insulting to the lady, but that was the longest hour of my life, and if I never hear mention of the word 'ribbon' again, it will be too soon."

"Really?" Letty gestured to Vander's coat, which was exquisitely tailored in dove grey superfine, emphasizing his broad shoulders and trim waist. "You are widely regarded as a tastemaker when it comes to fashion. I would have thought you could tolerate a discussion of millinery."

"I can, just not one that lasts for a full hour. For my next candidate, I would appreciate it if you could choose a woman who has more than one topic of conversation and who occasionally pauses for breath."

Letty fanned herself more brusquely, annoyed. "I asked what qualities you were looking for, and you said *beautiful*. So, I gave you beautiful."

"You did, but I would now like to amend my request. I require a bride who is beautiful *and* intelligent."

Letty slumped against the black velvet squabs. She couldn't decide whether she was annoyed that Vander had found her suggestion—which was *precisely what he had asked for*—lacking, or relieved that she would not have to watch him marry Priscilla Peabody. Perhaps a bit of both. "Fine. Let me think on it tonight. I'll send you a note once I've arranged a meeting with someone else."

"Thank you." He nudged her with his elbow. She glanced up and found him grinning his scoundrel's grin down at her.

Her annoyance shriveled. It was truly impossible to remain mad at this man.

"So, how did you fare with Throckmorton?" he asked.

"Better, I think, than you did with Miss Peabody," she said carefully.

Vander snorted. "Not the most ringing endorsement."

She squeezed her eyes shut. "Unlike you, I cannot just throw my suitors out and ask for new candidates. I must choose between the two men who have asked me. Lord Throckmorton does not seem like a bad man. Who knows? Perhaps, with time, we would come to have a very agreeable marriage."

"Hmmm." Vander sounded distinctly unimpressed. "Have you kissed him?"

Letty fumbled her fan, managing to drop it. "Have I *what*?"

"Have you kissed him?" Vander took his eyes off the horses for an instant. Whatever he saw on her face—panic, most likely— made him roll his eyes. "This is no time to be missish. Whichever man you choose, there's a good chance he'll be the only man you'll kiss—and do *other things* with—for the rest of your life. Compatibility is important. Trust me."

Letty's cheeks were aflame as she retrieved her fan from the phaeton's floor. "I—I know that," she sputtered. "I'm just shocked that you want to speak about such a grossly inappropriate topic."

Vander laughed. "This is *me*, Letty. The most scandalous man in London. Grossly inappropriate topics are my specialty. But, in all seriousness, I've decided to help you pick amongst your suitors. It seems the least I can do, given the lengths you're going to on my behalf. Now, as I was saying, however unseemly it may be, compatibility when it comes to, er, *kissing*, is crucial. As you clearly haven't made any forays in that direction—"

"I *have*," Letty hissed. "I'm not an idiot. If you must know, I have kissed them both."

She thought Vander would crow at having been proved right. But strangely, a sour look stole over his face, just for an instant. He shook his head, and his expression cleared. "Er—excellent. It's only sensible, after all. So, which one is better at kissing?"

"Better?" Letty looked away, watching rows of shops pass by in a blur. This was the question she'd been turning over in her head far too often, and still, she was unsure of the answer.

"Bertie's kiss was very"—she waved a hand, searching for the term—"*wet*. And Lord Throckmorton's was quite... *dry*."

"So, they're both terrible at kissing," Vander said, swinging his team into a turn.

Letty fanned her burning cheeks. "I didn't say that!"

"And yet, you did." He cut his eyes to her. "Have you ever had a decent kiss?"

Letty glanced to the side, wondering how badly she would injure herself were she to leap from the moving carriage in an attempt to escape this conversation.

Probably quite badly. They were a good six feet off the ground.

"They are the only two men I have ever kissed," she answered stiffly.

"That does make the situation challenging," Vander mused. At her confused look, he added, "It takes some time to get to know a new partner. Everyone is different and will have certain things they like and others they don't care for. What I'm trying to say is, they might be trainable. But it would help if you had more experience, so you could show them what you like."

They were pulling into Grosvenor Square, where the Baldridge townhouse was located. Letty's time with Vander was drawing to a close. "That seems rather unlikely," she noted.

"Perhaps so." Vander reined in the horses. "Well, you can at least"—he wrinkled his nose, an expression of distaste coming across his features—"try again, and see if either of them improves with practice."

Letty gave an involuntary shudder, a gesture she wished wasn't so telling. "I'll see what I can do."

Vander hopped down, then helped her descend to the pavement. He saw her to the door and was back atop his conveyance in a moment, driving away without a single glance back.

Letty sighed as she peered through the curtains in the front room, watching until he disappeared from sight. She knew already that she would think about him all evening.

Shaking her head, she let the curtains fall back into place and headed upstairs to change for dinner.

Chapter Eight

Around three o'clock in the morning, Vander found himself at Boodle's, seated at a round table with five other men. The game was brag, and Vander was winning.

He could've been winning more if he'd sat at Lord Waplington's table. The earl, who was second cousin to his father, and around his father's age, was terrible at brag, or any form of cards, really.

But Waplington was one of those tiresome fellows who was always complimenting Vander for speaking English so well or trying to explain what a phaeton was (as if Vander didn't own two of them). Attempts to remind him that Vander had been born in London and had never set foot in India were, in Vander's experience, fruitless.

"You probably won't like this," Waplington had once said when the beefsteak Vander had ordered came out. "It's much less spicy than what you people are used to."

Vander tried to follow his mother's advice, which was, "We must ignore these idiots." His parents kept an Indian chef in addition to a French one, so he had grown up enjoying a variety of foods with actual flavor. But, having attended both Eton and Cambridge, he had eaten every joint of meat known to man, and even liked them, so long as they hadn't been boiled into oblivion.

When David was there, he could at least make a joke about it under his breath. "Waplington probably subsists on boiled ham."

"Boiled mutton," David would respond with a grin. "He finds ham terribly spicy."

But David wasn't here tonight, and Vander didn't think he had the strength to grimace through an evening at Lord Waplington's table without him. He had therefore ignored the open chair next to the earl and found another in the back of the card room.

Brag was a simple game. The players were dealt three cards each, and the only decision one had to make was whether to stay in or to fold. When he determined he was going to try his hand at earning a living at the gaming tables, Vander had spent an afternoon calculating the odds that any given hand would be the highest one dealt. He now knew, roughly, where he stood on each and every hand, and whether it was worth his while to play or to fold. He folded more frequently than the other men at the table, but his careful strategy was paying off—Vander now had more chips than any of his fellows.

He glanced around as the dealer swept up the last batch of cards. Being here without David was... different. Not as enjoyable, he had to acknowledge.

It wasn't merely that he missed his friend's company. Being here alone, he had more time to observe the other men in the room, and Vander was having trouble deciding where he fit in. There were the young bloods, loud and boisterous, experiencing London for the first time. That had been David and him five years ago, but looking at them now... they seemed so *young*. So immature. Vander realized that he no longer fit in with that group and that he never would again.

That left the older men, like Lord Brentwood, who was seated to his right. Brentwood was a solid player, perhaps not as technically precise as Vander, but with a good general sense of the odds, having played most every night for decades.

Vander supposed Brentwood was what he was aspiring to. He probably won more than he lost, and he was too sensible to ever lose his shirt. But, watching the earl, he seemed a bit... bored. He had looked pleased earlier when he drew a flush, but overall, Vander didn't get the sense that he was *enjoying* himself.

Then there was Francis Llewellyn. Francis was around Vander's age, maybe a year or two younger. He didn't know him well, as Francis had attended Oxford, while Vander had gone to Cambridge.

Llewellyn didn't play well at all. He didn't have a stoic bone in his body; whether his cards were good or bad, you could read it on his face. He didn't have a good grasp of the odds and would bet large sums on middling hands. With a better player, Vander would've assumed he was bluffing, but Francis Llewellyn couldn't bluff if his life depended on it. He'd had one lucky hand, so he was only down about twenty pounds, but as his losses slowly grew, he became increasingly ill at ease.

"There you are, gents," the dealer said, distributing another round of cards. Vander glanced at his hand and had to fight to keep his features neutral. He'd just been dealt a straight flush, in the form of the eight, nine, and ten of spades.

It was an extraordinarily good hand. Only a prial, three-of-a-kind, could beat a straight flush. Vander had spent last night going over the odds, which meant that he knew that there were 22,100 possible hands in the game of brag.

Out of those 22,100 possible hands, only seventy-two could beat the cards Vander had been dealt.

The odds that he would lose this hand were less than one percent.

Strictly speaking, they were 0.32579 percent.

Not that Vander would ever say as much. That was the sort of thing a quiz would say.

The dealer turned to Brentwood. "Your bet, my lord."

"I fold." Brentwood's eyes met Vander's, and he knew instinctively that the earl had seen the surprise flash across his face when he saw his cards. He would have to be more careful in the future.

The betting came to Llewellyn, who was shifting in his seat, excitement palpable on his face. He obviously liked his hand, too. "Here," he said, shoving five chips into the pot.

It was rich for a starting bet, and the other men groaned. One by one, when play passed to them, they folded.

All save Vander, of course.

After Llewellyn ran out of chips, he tossed his pocket watch onto the pile.

"That's worth what, fifty pounds?" Vander asked.

Brentwood picked it up, examining it. "Thirty," he grunted.

Vander put in some more chips. By now Llewellyn's cheeks were red, and he had to wipe his palms on his trousers. "I'll stake my carriage," he said tightly.

Vander called for two hundred pounds' worth of chips, which were brought to him at once. Everyone knew he was good for it.

"And my team," Llewellyn added.

Vander removed his sapphire stickpin and tossed it into the pot.

Llewellyn's brow creased. "You don't want to fold?"

As the stakes grew richer, Vander had been contemplating just that. Although it wasn't likely, maybe Llewellyn had been dealt one of those seventy-two hands that would beat Vander's straight flush.

0.32579 percent, he reminded himself.

If he didn't have the guts to stay in at 0.32579 percent, he didn't have any business being here.

"No," Vander said, "but why don't we show?"

Llewellyn shook his head. "I've a thousand pounds cash in the bank," he said quickly. At Vander's surprised look, he added, "It's to pay for my commission. I'll be joining the Tenth Light Dragoons."

Vander winced. "Are you sure you want to stake that?"

"Yes," Llewellyn said tightly.

A crowd had begun to gather, as their table had by far the deepest play at the moment. "All right," Vander said. "But then we show."

Llewellyn nodded tightly. Vander requested more chips—a huge pile this time. The room had gone silent as everyone waited for the reveal.

Llewellyn flipped his cards over first. Vander held his breath as he leaned forward to see that Llewellyn had—

A pair of sixes?

Vander couldn't believe it. It wasn't that a pair of sixes was a bad hand. A pair of sixes would beat just over eighty percent of all other possible hands.

But you didn't bet the money you needed to buy your commission on *a pair of sixes.*

Beside him, Brentwood was shaking his head.

"Well?" Llewellyn said, and Vander realized he had left everyone in suspense. Feeling guilty, he flipped over his cards...

... and the room exploded. It wasn't every night someone drew a straight flush, and to see it happen on such a rich hand was the reason men came to Boodle's. People were slapping him on the back, congratulating him.

Vander tried to catch Llewellyn's eye across the table. His gaze was fixed on the tablecloth.

He should have felt elated. This was what he had come here to do, after all—see if he could make a living by gambling. And he had just earned over fifteen hundred pounds on one hand! It should have been a triumph.

But, watching Llewellyn blink rapidly, then wipe his nose with the heel of his hand... Vander knew the man was fighting back tears.

Money lost at the tables was a debt of honor. Absolutely no one would fault Vander for holding Llewellyn to his word, even though, so far as they knew, Vander was one of the richest men in London, a man who could afford to use ten-pound bank notes to light his cheroots, should he feel so inclined, while Llewellyn had possibly just ruined his life.

But it happened that Vander did need this money if he was going to get out from under his father's thumb. And so, he couldn't afford to punch Llewellyn in the shoulder, take his chips and his pocket watch, and tell him to keep the rest of it, and for the love of God, don't bet your commission money on a bloody pair of sixes.

"A round of drinks," Vander declared, his voice sounding hollow to his own ears. "A round of drinks for the room." Because this was what he was expected to do. He needed to be well-liked so people would keep playing with him. He wasn't worried about tonight. He'd been dealt a lucky hand, and it didn't take a genius to know that you don't fold on a straight flush.

But at some point, people would realize that he wasn't just a little bit lucky. The time to prepare for that day was now.

As the waiters scurried to open some more bottles, Vander watched Llewellyn slip from the room, shoulders slumped.

Vander's plan was a marvelous success.

So why, he wondered as he plucked a glass from a passing tray, wasn't he happy about it?

Chapter Nine

After a scant three hours of sleep, Vander presented himself at Beauclerk Marine Casualty, as demanded by his father.

The company offices were located on a nondescript street in the parish of St. George in the East. The London Docks were nearby. So was the Tower of London, not that there was a view of either from the narrow brick building sandwiched in a row of middling storefronts.

The room his father had left him in did have a window, but the buildings in this neighborhood were packed so tightly that little sunlight trickled through it, and the dimness of the room compounded the temptation to lay his head down on the desk and sleep.

God, what he would give for a decent cup of coffee...

The door burst open, and his father scurried into the room. Unlike the dozen clerks Vander had passed on his way in, who looked to be waging a losing battle against lethargy, his father's eyes shone with excitement to be in his favorite place, his insurance office.

"So," his father said, taking a seat next to Vander at the bare wooden table. "Do you understand the policies I asked you to go over?"

Vander peeled off the spectacles he was careful never to wear in public. "Yes. And no."

His father crossed his legs. "What didn't you understand?"

"Two things." Vander shuffled through the pile of files before him, pulling out six. "These applications looked sound. Why did you decline to quote these policies?"

His father peered at the papers. "These ships are all bound for Callao. The route around Cape Horn is dangerous. I've done an analysis, and ships are lost there at three times the rate of, say, the Cape of Good Hope."

"So why don't we charge three times the rate?" Vander countered.

His father shook his head. "Who could afford to pay three times the rate?"

Vander thumped his hand against the table. "Guano farmers, that's who. Have you seen the prices Peruvian guano is fetching on the open market? It's a risky venture, but the potential rewards are substantial. And all six of these shipowners are trading in guano. Who usually insures this route?"

His father screwed up his face. "It's my understanding that no one will. Those ships usually sail uninsured."

Vander stood and stretched, then settled with a hip on the desk. "This route is an opportunity. There will be losses. Make no mistake. But if we price it right, and if we recruit enough clients to properly pool the risk, there's no reason we couldn't underwrite these policies."

His father frowned. "I don't know, Evander."

Vander smacked the papers with the back of his hand. "What was it you were saying to me the other day? About the sacred duty of insurers to mitigate risk so commerce can flow? Think of your king and your country. And of the bloody fortune Beauclerk Marine Casualty stands to make if we insure all of this bird shit."

The corners of his father's mouth quirked up.

"What's this?" Vander asked. "I didn't expect you to laugh at my bird-shit joke. I expected you to say"—he placed his hands on his hips and made his voice high and nasal—"*Evander! Don't be so crude.*"

His father laughed again, taking no offense. "It was crude, and I expect you to refrain from using such language in business settings. But that's actually not what made me smile." His father clasped his hands before him on the desk. "It's nice to hear you say *we*, with regards to Beauclerk Marine Casualty."

Vander sank back into his chair. This was probably his father's dream come true, to have his son here, learning the family business.

Little did he know that, if things went according to Vander's plan, this would only be a temporary interlude.

He set those thoughts aside. "We should quote these policies. If they don't like the rate we would have to charge, that's their prerogative. But at least we will have tried."

His father blinked at the stack of folios, his brow creased. "I'm not sure, Evander. But I will run the numbers one more time."

"Good."

"You said there was one more thing you didn't understand?"

"Yes." Vander put his spectacles back on as he took up a file he had set aside. "It's this policy, for the *Windermere*. Did the losses they reported last year not strike you as odd?"

His father leaned in to look at the policy. "What do you mean?"

"The *Windermere* set sail out of Bombay with a cargo of silks and spices." He peered at his father over the tops of his glasses. "Which immediately seems suspicious. Bombay isn't on the spice route. I wouldn't question it if the ship had made port in Calicut."

His father blinked, looking startled. "It does seem a bit odd, now that you mention it."

"It gets worse." Vander ran a finger down the policy, searching for the right passage. "Halfway through the voyage, they determined that the twenty-three chests of spices had gone moldy." He paused, glancing up at his father. "All twenty-three? Which were presumably sealed up tight? That seems—"

"Questionable," his father interjected, brow wrinkled.

"It seems bloody implausible. But that's not all—they determined that the best course to prevent the spread of mold to the ship's stores was to cast all twenty-three chests into the sea." Vander tossed the policy onto the table in front of him and leaned back in his chair. "Leaving not a shred of evidence to support their losses. That's awfully convenient. Meanwhile, it sounds like the ship's stores were unaffected. What are the odds that a tightly-sealed chest of pepper would become infested by mold, while an open crate of hard tack was fine?"

"Not very high," his father said, removing his glasses and rubbing the bridge of his nose. "But these are very serious accusations, Evander. And we have signed statements from the ship's officers attesting that this sequence of events, as unlikely as they may now seem, occurred. Surely, you're not suggesting that all of those men lied under oath?"

Vander sighed. His father might be extremely book smart, but he spent so much time hiding in his ivory tower, he could be alarmingly ignorant when it came to the ways of the world. It didn't help that his sense of honor was so deeply enshrined, he almost could not imagine that someone would defraud him.

"That's exactly what I'm suggesting, Father. Look at the facts. They make no sense."

His father shifted uncomfortably in his seat. "But... But..." Abruptly, he deflated, slumping down in his chair. "Oh, you're right. Of course, you are. I cannot believe they would have the gall to lie to me!" He sighed. "The evidence being circumstantial, I very much doubt we could prove the claim was fraudulent in court."

Vander leaned forward. "But we could decline to underwrite the *Windermere's* next voyage. And we should refuse to insure any ships under the same ownership."

His father made a sound of despair. "The owner would be furious. It would be like kicking a hornet's nest."

Vander pushed the file toward his father. "Still, it might be worth it. We don't want to work with liars."

"No. That we don't. Oh, botheration! The thought that someone would take advantage of me like this... I hope you will excuse my strong language, but it burns my buttons!" He sighed, putting his glasses back on. "I'll have to think about the best course."

"Please do. I know you'll do the right thing."

His father smiled as he stood. "You're good at this. A chip off the old block." He made a bent-wrist fist and bumped it awkwardly against Vander's shoulder.

Vander smiled. His father's bumbling attempt at camaraderie was strangely endearing. "Thank you, Father."

His father scooped up the files they had discussed and started toward the door. "I'll bring you some more policies to go over this afternoon."

"That will have to wait until tomorrow. This afternoon, I will be visiting the British Museum."

His father frowned. "If you want to run a successful business, you can't just take off whenever it pleases you. I'll have you know I put in twelve-hour days, at the very least!"

That was precisely why Vander wasn't cut out to run Beau-clerk Marine Casualty, even though he was finding the risk analysis element of the business more interesting than he had expected.

He held up both hands. "You're the one who wanted me to marry a respectable woman by month's end. That's why I'm going to the British Museum—Letty is going to introduce me to someone."

His father's expression remained surly.

Vander laughed. "Come, Father. How am I supposed to meet a likely young lady if I'm cooped up in here for twelve hours a day?"

His father's rigid stance softened. "I suppose you have a point," he grumbled.

"Don't worry, all this"—Vander gestured to the stack of policies he had yet to read through—"will still be here tomorrow."

"Very well," his father said, taking his leave.

The door did not swing closed after him, as Vander's cousin, Milton, appeared in its frame. "Vander! I—I heard you were here." Milton pointed toward the front office where the dozen clerks in his father's employ had their desks. "H-how have you been?"

Considering he'd been featured in the *Rake Review* and was now being forced into a life he detested, not so well. But Milton didn't need to know that, so Vander said, "Fine. Just fine. How've you been, Milton?"

"Grand!" Milton said with an unconvincing attempt at enthusiasm. "I, uh, I was just wondering if you might like to join me for lunch. Seeing as we haven't caught up in, you know. A while."

Milton was wringing his hands, and based on his cringing posture, Vander suspected he was bracing himself for rejection.

But Vander was already on his feet. There were few excuses he wouldn't take to get out of this dismal cave of a room. "I'd like that."

Milton's eyes had gone wide behind his spectacles. "You would? I mean... w-wonderful. Let me just get my hat and we can, uh... You know."

They went to a chop house around the corner. After they'd put in their orders, Vander turned to his cousin. "So. How have things been with—"

"Look, Vander," Milton said in a rush, "I know you probably

think I'm an idiot. That I'm dumber than a bucket of turnips. That I'm the biggest simpleton this side of the—"

"Milton!" Vander gave an awkward chuckle, attempting to wave off the dozen curious faces who had swiveled in their direction. In truth, Milton wasn't entirely wrong, but even Vander wasn't tactless enough to mention it.

Vander tried to make his expression innocent. "Why would you say such a thing?"

Blotches of red stained Milton's cheeks. "I saw how many errors there were on the ledgers I attempted. I know you were the one who corrected them. I recognized your handwriting."

Vander inclined his head, figuring it was better not to deny it. "I mean... everyone makes mistakes."

"You don't," Milton grumbled, nodding his thanks to the waiter as he set a pork chop before him. "And now your father probably thinks I'm going to ruin his beloved business."

Vander snorted, taking up his knife and fork and slicing his beefsteak. "Oh, I make mistakes, all right." At Milton's skeptical look, he acknowledged, "Not so much when it comes to ledgers and the like. But I made a sufficient bungle of the rest of my life that I managed to get featured in the *Rake Review*."

Milton rolled his eyes. "Oh, yes. How awful. Now the whole world knows that women are desperate to spend the night in your bed and swoon every time you take off your shirt, to say nothing of the fact that you were third wrangler."

"Yes, well, it also said I have the attention span of a gnat, *and* that I have the pox." Vander pointed with his fork. "Which, for the record, I do *not*."

One corner of Milton's mouth quirked up. "I guess the article wasn't entirely fawning."

Vander speared a potato forcefully. "No. No, it was not. And as to your assertion that my father thinks you'll ruin the family business"—he laughed darkly—"I'm the one doing that."

Milton frowned. "How so?"

Vander explained what his father had told him about policy-holders fleeing. "Father has given me one month to marry and start leading a respectable life." Vander shoved his plate, the contents of which didn't seem nearly as appetizing as they had five minutes ago, out of the way. "My life is over."

Milton huffed. "It won't be that bad. You'll be able to marry your pick of the most beautiful women in London. And I've never understood why you're so averse to Beauclerk Marine Casualty."

Vander paused, wiping a drip of condensation from his pint of ale. "It's not that I'm averse to it, precisely. Learning the business hasn't been as bad as I expected. The risk analysis side of it is actually rather interesting. But I don't want to do it to the exclusion of everything else, the way my father does. To spend twelve hours a day stuffed in a closet and never see the sun."

"I like being at the office," Milton sighed. "It makes me feel important. All I've ever wanted is to be a successful businessman, like your father. Now he's probably going to dismiss me."

"He's not, Milton. He's really not," Vander insisted, hating the hangdog expression on his cousin's face. "The thing is, you're responsible. My father trusts you. At this point, I think the odds are better that he leaves Beauclerk Marine Casualty to you than to me."

"That will never happen," Milton muttered.

Vander studied his cousin. He and Milton were close enough in age that they should've been close growing up. But they weren't. This was the deepest conversation they'd had in... maybe ever.

"I hope this doesn't come off the wrong way," Vander began. "But I'm genuinely curious—you obviously tried hard in school. And you're not stupid—you're not," Vander insisted when Milton started to interrupt him. "So, I'm wondering why you struggled so much with those ledgers. Do you think it could be nerves? Perhaps you're so eager to impress my father that you get overwhelmed?"

"It's not nerves. It's worse than that." Milton glanced around. "Do you want to know the truth?"

Vander nodded, and they both leaned forward.

"I'm so thick, I can't even read all of the numbers correctly," Milton whispered. "It's hard for me to distinguish between the sixes and the nines. There are certain letters I mix up, too—b's and d's." Milton shook his head. "I'm just an idiot."

"No," Vander said quickly. "Stop saying that. I—I've never heard of that before. But let's try something."

He plucked one of Milton's pencils from his waistcoat pocket and grabbed a morning paper someone had left behind. In the margin, Vander wrote out a column of numbers, none of which included a six or a nine.

He spun the paper around to face Milton and slapped the pencil down. "Add that up. Go on."

Milton cringed, but he took up the pencil and went to work. He was a bit slow about it, although perhaps that wasn't fair. Everyone was slower at sums than Vander, excepting his father.

But Milton got the answer right. He glanced up at Vander, looking terrified he had made a mistake.

Vander grinned. "That's right."

Milton's shoulders sagged with relief. "It is?"

Vander laughed. "It is. See, you're not stupid. Not at all." He held up his thumb and index finger, pinched a sliver apart. "There's just one tiny part of your brain that's, how you say—"

"Broken," Milton supplied. A harsh word, but at least there was a ghost of a smile upon his lips.

"Not the word I was going to use. But it's like I said—no one's good at everything. Look at all the things you're good at that I'm not. Rising before noon. Showing up at the office. Not sleeping with half the opera dancers in London."

Milton laughed out loud, and Vander grinned. "It's a shame

ONE FINE MAY

we can't combine our brains," Vander said. "I feel like together, we would make one fully functioning person."

Milton smiled, and it reached his bespectacled eyes. "Thank you, Vander."

"Of course." Vander signaled to the waiter and took care of the bill, ignoring Milton's attempts to insist that it was his treat.

Milton headed back to the offices, but Vander hailed a hackney carriage. As it bore him toward the British Museum, he was eager to see what sort of young lady Letty had for him today.

Chapter Ten

L etty waited in the gallery of the British Museum, wondering which of the people she'd invited would be the first to arrive.

She had invited three—Vander, Bertie Strickleton, and Miss Mathilda Seymour. Letty had thought long and hard about which young lady best met Vander's request for someone both clever and beautiful, finally deciding upon Mathilda. Mathilda was the granddaughter of the Duke of Harrowgate. Her father, one of the duke's younger sons, had been granted a lucrative church living near the family seat in Yorkshire. The area was apparently riddled with artifacts, both Viking and Roman, and Mathilda had a reputation for being a keen student of both archeology and history.

She was also lovely, with curling brown hair and fine, dark eyes. Mathilda wasn't generally considered to be a diamond of the first water, but Letty thought this was only due to her reserved nature. As the granddaughter of a duke, her social connections were impeccable, but as the daughter of a younger son, her dowry was small, which was a barrier to many men who might otherwise have been interested.

But, of course, that was no obstacle for the likes of Vander.

As if she had summoned him, Vander appeared in the doorway to the gallery, looking heart-stoppingly handsome in a midnight-blue coat and cream silk waistcoat, his dark silken hair fashionably rumpled atop his head. He smiled lazily as he crossed the gallery and Letty felt as though she might melt into a puddle upon the floor.

He gave an elegant half-bow. "Letty."

She curtseyed in return. "Vander."

He offered his arm, and they began strolling the length of the gallery. It was one of the handful of days each month when anyone who was "respectably dressed" was permitted to look around the museum without one of the museum's officers rushing them through the exhibits.

"How was your morning?" Vander asked.

"Fine. Uneventful," Letty replied. "How was yours?"

Vander pursed his lips, thinking. "Not nearly as bad as I feared. I've been at my father's offices."

"Ah. And how are you enjoying the world of insurance?"

Vander drew them to a halt before a headless statue of Zeus. "That's the thing—the insurance part of it is surprisingly interesting. It's all the rest of it that's intolerable."

Letty tilted her head, studying him. He looked genuinely troubled. "What do you mean by 'all the rest of it?'"

"My father spends upward of twelve hours a day at the office," Vander said, resuming their progress. "That's including Sundays. More, when things are busy. And the office in question is a glorified closet whose few windows look out on a view of a gloomy alley."

Letty hummed sympathetically. "It doesn't sound as if I would want to spend my days there, either. But you could move the business to a different location. Do you think your father would consider it?"

Vander frowned. "I don't know. I've never asked him. Certainly, he could afford to rent some nicer offices."

"If you find it so dismal, surely his clerks do, too. A move would boost morale. You could frame it for him that way."

"You know, I believe I will. A better view would make the whole prospect less grim." He drew them to a halt and nudged Letty with his elbow. "Speaking of impressive views, how do you fancy this one?"

He had stopped before a Roman statue depicting a discus thrower winding up to make his toss. A completely *naked* discus thrower. His arms were sculpted in more ways than one, and rows of muscles stretched across his torso. Why, there was even a dimple in his... nether regions!

Letty felt her cheeks flushing, but she lifted her chin. "Do *you* find this view impressive? Why, Vander—I had no idea."

He chuckled. "Well played, Letty. It is finely executed." A wicked gleam came into his eyes. "Even if I would prefer for the subject to be—"

"I have a fair idea what subjects you prefer," Letty said crisply. "We all do, after reading the *Rake Review*."

"There goes my air of mystery." Vander gave a theatrical sigh, then looped his arm through Letty's and resumed their stroll. "So. Who will I be meeting today?"

"Miss Mathilda Seymour." Letty gave him a quick summary of Miss Seymour's situation and interests. "I think you will find that she is precisely what you have requested."

Just then, Letty spied Miss Seymour in the doorway to the gallery. "Ah, here she is."

Vander made a hum of interest. "She looks promising."

Tamping down the stab of jealousy that shot through her, Letty led Vander down the gallery. They met Miss Seymour halfway.

"Miss Seymour," Letty said, "may I present Mr. Evander Beauclerk?"

Vander took her hand and gave her a charming smile. "Miss Seymour, what a pleasure."

Mathilda blushed ferociously as he bowed over her hand. Although her material situation was not as desperate as that of Miss Peabody, if she hoped to marry, she needed a man rich enough that her minuscule dowry was no impediment, which constrained her options considerably. She had therefore responded with a stammering sort of enthusiasm when Letty offered to introduce her to Vander, asking with a touch of wonder if he had really been third wrangler at Cambridge.

They made small talk for a few minutes. The topic moved to the archaeological digs Mathilda had seen in Yorkshire. "In fact," Mathilda said, "some Roman artifacts from Ribchester have recently been put on display. I would quite like to see them."

This, of course, was Letty's signal to take her leave. The clock had already chimed the quarter of an hour. Where could Bertie be? Of all the times to be late...

Miss Seymour's smile encompassed both Vander and Letty. She seemed to be under the impression that they would be making up a party of three. "Shall we?"

Letty held up her hands, taking a step back in alarm. "I wouldn't want to intrude." She wasn't about to make a gooseberry of herself. "I'm actually meeting someone."

Vander, who had already offered one arm to Mathilda, held the other one out toward her. "It's all right, Letty. Join us."

Watching Vander spend the next hour charming another woman was about the last thing Letty wanted to do. Why couldn't Bertie be on time for once? "No, really, the person I'm waiting for is—"

"Letty! There you are!" Bertie chose that moment to come bounding into the gallery. "I'm not late, am I? What time is it?"

Up and down the gallery, heads swiveled in their direction in response to Bertie's enthusiastic tone, which would have been fine at the pall-mall game the other day but reverberated down the length of the quiet gallery.

Unaware of the censorious looks he was attracting, Bertie

seized Letty's hand and pressed three lingering kisses to its back. Embarrassed, Letty sought to extract her hand without making it look like a reproach.

Burying her hands in her skirts to prevent Bertie from seizing them again, she turned to her companions. "Mr. Strickleton, I believe you are acquainted with Miss Mathilda Seymour and Mr. Evander Beauclerk?"

"Course I am." Bertie nodded to Miss Seymour, then seized Vander's hand and pumped it. "Miss Seymour. Beauclerk."

Miss Seymour looked startled by Bertie's whirlwind entrance. Vander was openly scowling at him, not that Bertie seemed to notice. He seized Letty's arm so suddenly that he pulled her off balance. She chuckled weakly in an attempt to cover her discomfiture.

"Right," Bertie said, nodding to the other couple. "If you'll excuse us, then."

"Bertie," Letty whispered as he propelled her down the gallery. "Do slow d—"

"You'll never believe who called on me this morning," Bertie interrupted. "Figgy Ganderton! I haven't seen old Figgy in three whole weeks, on account of him going to visit his aunt up in Norfolk. As you can imagine, we had loads to discuss."

Letty smiled apologetically at a matron who was glaring at Bertie through her lorgnette. "How wonderful, that you were able to catch up with your friend," she said, pitching her voice at a whisper. She considered their destination. If Vander and Mathilda were heading to the rooms containing Roman artifacts, she didn't want to go within a thousand yards of them. "Could we head toward the Egyptian rooms? I would quite like to see the Rosetta—"

"And then," Bertie boomed, "who should walk in but Hugo Chegwidden! Why, I haven't seen Cheggers in at least five days, quite possibly six! Naturally, a celebration was in order."

"Naturally." As Bertie did not appear to be picking up on her cues, she decided a change in strategy was called for. "Would you like to see the gardens? I quite fancy a stroll around the gardens."

Bertie gave no sign of having heard her. "We rounded up Batty McCorkindale and Francis Ditherington and set out to make a day of it."

The one good thing about Bertie's lack of awareness about their general surroundings was that he allowed her to steer him down the stairs, out the door, and into the museum's gardens. It took eleven circuits of the garden's graveled path for him to work his excitement at having spent the morning with his friends out of his system. "And once we finished fencing, I said, crikey, would you look at the time—I'm due to meet Letty at the British Museum! And that is why I was a few minutes late. So." He gave her a lazy grin. "How are you?"

Before Letty could respond, an elderly woman wearing an emerald green turban marched up to Bertie. "Young man! Do keep your voice down. There was a great spotted woodpecker in that pear tree that we were observing. Then you came along, all but shouting, and frightened it away!"

Bertie's face fell. "Did I truly?" He looked to Letty for confirmation, and she nodded. He turned back to the woman in the turban. "Gosh, I'm terribly sorry."

Letty sighed as Bertie submitted contritely to the woman's lecture. This was his redeeming feature. Bertie truly meant well, and he didn't have a cruel bone in his body. But he was oblivious to the point that the outcome was the same—a casual discourteousness for those around him that left Letty feeling embarrassed.

He reminded her of a beagle she'd had as a child—a boundless well of enthusiasm that often led to disaster and broken crockery.

Of course, Patches had grown out of it after a couple of years.

Bertie was now two and twenty, and he showed no signs that he was heading in a similar direction.

Still, no one could have a better nature than Bertie, who even now was bowing deeply to the lady who had reproached him. "I apologize most sincerely. Thank you ever so much for bringing it to my attention. I will endeavor to do better, I promise."

It was impossible to maintain an angry mien in the face of such sincerity. "Yes, well... See to it that you do." The woman patted his hand firmly. "Good day, young man."

Bertie turned to Letty, rubbing the back of his head. "I can't believe I did that. I tell you what—if I start to get too loud again, I want you to stomp on my foot as hard as you can to get my attention."

Letty didn't much relish the image of herself doing something so uncouth in public. "How about if I just tell you?"

Bertie screwed up his face. "I suppose that could work."

"Very good." Letty gave him a tight smile. "Would you like to go inside and look at the Egyptian antiquities?"

"A wonderful suggestion," Bertie said, offering his arm. As he led her back inside, he bent his head close to her ear. "You'll never believe who I bumped into last night..."

Letty's smile was drawn as Bertie launched into the story. Well, at least this time he was whispering.

Chapter Eleven

Inside the rooms containing Roman artifacts, Vander was bored out of his skull.

It wasn't that Miss Seymour was a poor conversationalist. She was miles better than Priscilla Peabody.

But if a topic existed in which they shared a mutual interest, Vander had yet to discover it.

Miss Seymour had seemed promising at first. As they made their way to the Roman rooms, she explained, "The Ribchester Hoard was discovered a few years before I was born. A little boy, a clog maker's son, was digging in the mud by a river and happened upon it." She gestured to a glass case. "Can you even imagine stumbling upon something so magnificent?"

It was an intriguing vignette, and Vander felt a keen sense of anticipation as he leaned forward and peered into the case. Most of it was badly rusted bits and bobs, but there was a helmet that was still impressive after more than a thousand years. It looked more like a statue than a helmet, with a finely sculpted face with tiny slits for the eyes, nose, and mouth. A hole had rusted through where the forehead used to be, but otherwise, it was in remarkably fine condition.

At this point, Vander was feeling positively optimistic about Mathilda Seymour. He'd asked Letty for a woman who was both clever and beautiful, and she certainly fit the bill. If it came down to it, he could stand to be married to her.

He admired the helmet for a couple of minutes, then glanced at Miss Seymour to see if she was ready to move on.

She was not.

Mathilda Seymour was just getting started.

She oohed over the metal guards that had once protected a horse's eyes from stray spears. Those looked like colanders. She aahed over a rusty old frying pan. Which looked like... every frying pan Vander had ever seen. And she cooed over every corroding scrap of metal inside the glass-topped display cabinet the way most women cooed over the jewelry case at Rundell and Bridge.

It wasn't that Vander disliked the Ribchester Hoard. But he was ready to move on after five minutes, while Miss Seymour seemed prepared to stand there for the next five hours.

She noticed his waning enthusiasm and immediately suggested they go and see something else. An awkward dance ensued, in which he insisted she stay and examine the artifacts, as days like this, when visitors were permitted to take their time, were few and far between, and she insisted they move on, as she could tell he was bored. In the end, they spent ten minutes debating the point in painfully polite tones before Vander finally yielded to her insistence that they see something else, and neither of them was happy.

They passed the sculpture of the discus thrower, the same one Vander had teased Letty about earlier. He pressed Miss Seymour's arm and made his voice suggestive. "What do you think about this one?"

Her cheeks turned scarlet, and she dropped her gaze to the floor. "It is... er... in very fine condition for its age."

That sealed it. Any woman who was going to spend a lifetime with him needed to possess a high tolerance—no, an *enjoyment*—

of ribald jokes. If such a mild insinuation sent Miss Seymour blushing and stammering, there was no possibility that they would rub on well together.

Still, he had to pass another hour in her company, so Vander tried to make the best of it. Miss Seymour tried, too. At one point, she eagerly asked about his time at Cambridge, and if he had truly been third wrangler. This, of course, was the last thing Vander wanted to discuss, but she seemed to be laboring under the misapprehension that he had been a diligent student. He supposed most third wranglers were the types of men who would relish the chance to relive their glory days in academia, and Miss Seymour seemed to misinterpret his eagerness to change the subject as a becoming modesty.

When they came to the Egyptian artifacts, he spied Letty at the far end of the room. She was on Strickleton's arm, and his head was bent low, whispering in her ear.

Vander felt his stomach boil. Strickleton was clearly all wrong for her. He wasn't even good-looking unless one liked the boyish, blue-eyed, golden-haired type.

All right. In the interest of honesty, Vander had to acknowledge that Strickleton was considered to be a beau. Even if he didn't find it very manly to walk around looking like a bloody cherubim. But more importantly, Strickleton couldn't provide properly for Letty. Why, the fortune he was set to inherit from his uncle was rumored to only produce around five thousand a year!

Although... for just about everyone other than Vander, that was considered to be a fine income that could support a perfectly respectable lifestyle.

But surely Letty didn't *like* the man. What was there to like?

Across the gallery, Letty smiled up at her companion. Strickleton beamed at her in return. She squeezed his arm, and they wandered over toward a black stone sarcophagus.

Vander's shoulders sagged. In truth, Strickleton was a good sort of fellow and would probably make Letty a fine husband. She would be a thousand times better off being married to Bertie Strickleton than to the likes of him.

Good God—where had *that* thought come from? Vander wasn't considering marrying *Letty*. The very notion was absurd!

Although... he'd wanted someone clever, and Letty was clever. And he'd asked for someone beautiful. And... he couldn't believe he was thinking this, but now that it had come to his attention that she was no longer ten years old, he could not help but observe that she was in possession of some very fine, very delicate curves, and that when she smiled—not the serene smile she was giving Strickleton right now, but the impish grin she wore when she was ribbing Vander—her brown eyes sparkled, and she was as dazzling as any woman in London.

Dear Lord—what was *wrong* with him? He couldn't marry Letty! David would murder him if he so much as looked at her. And Letty deserved better than a cad like him, a man who was so dissolute he'd been featured in the *Rake Review*, for God's sake.

Letty deserved a prince on a white horse. She deserved—

A rich chuckle echoed down the gallery. Vander saw that Letty and Strickleton had their heads bent together, laughing at some jest.

She deserved someone like Bertie Strickleton.

"Mr. Beauclerk? Mr. Beauclerk?"

Vander shook himself, realizing he had been ignoring Miss Seymour for an inexcusable duration.

She gave him a tight smile. "Shall we take a look at the statue across the way? I believe it is of Rameses the Second..."

Vander spent another hour struggling to focus on Miss Seymour and the exhibits, then the two couples gathered at the entrance to take their leave.

Strickleton pressed a lingering kiss against the back of Letty's glove. The urge to punch him in his upturned nose grew overwhelming, so Vander clasped his hands behind his back.

"Will I see you tonight?" Strickleton asked, his eyes fixed upon Letty.

"I don't know," she said, looking flustered. "Will you be attending Lady Waldegrave's ball?"

Strickleton's face fell. "I won't. Mrs. Heathecote is hosting a dinner, and I promised Mama I would attend."

"Oh, that's too bad." It might have been Vander's imagination, but Letty didn't look too put out by this news. In fact, if he didn't know better, he would've said that she perked up a bit.

"We'll be going to Vauxhall tomorrow night," Letty offered. "Perhaps I'll see you there."

Strickleton pressed another wet kiss to the back of Letty's glove. "You may count upon it, Letty."

They handed the ladies into their respective carriages. Strickleton wished Vander a cheerful, "Good afternoon."

All Vander could manage was a grunt in return before he turned on heel and climbed into a hackney of his own.

So, Letty would be at Lady Waldegrave's ball. Not that this information mattered a whit, because Vander would not be in attendance. He needed to head over to Boodle's to continue his gambling experiment, and then his father was expecting him at Beauclerk Marine Casualty bright and early the next morning.

He would have to send Letty a note conveying his impression of Miss Seymour and describing what he would like to see in his next prospective bride because he was not going to be seeing her tonight at Lady Waldegrave's ball.

Of course, he wasn't.

Chapter Twelve

Vander's mother smiled at him as they strode into Lady Waldegrave's ballroom. "This is such a treat, Vander. It's not every day that you accompany me to a ball."

"Surely it's not that rare," Vander said, scanning the room. They had arrived fashionably late, as was his mother's habit, and it was already close to midnight. Letty could be anywhere by now...

"You do sometimes appear for five minutes in order to collect one of your friends, no doubt to drag him off to someplace much seedier. But I can count on one hand the number of times you stayed long enough to dance. Speaking of which"—she tugged on his arm, pulling him sharply to the right, and abruptly switched from Persian to English—"Letty, my dear! There you are."

Letty, who was standing near the refreshment table with her friend, Emily, stepped forward and kissed his mother on the cheek. "Good evening, Mrs. Beauclerk. You remember my friend Emily, don't you?"

"Of course, of course! Miss Arbuthnot, so lovely to see you again. And may I offer my congratulations on your engagement to Lord Trundley?"

Emily curtseyed deeply. "Thank you so much, Mrs. Beauclerk."

His mother pressed her bejeweled fan against her heart. "A wedding is such a wonderful thing! Are you having a new gown made for the ceremony? How dearly I should like to hear about your plans."

"And how dearly I love to talk about them!" Emily looped her arm through his mother's, pulling her from Vander's side. "I'm sure I've bored Letty to tears, nattering on about flowers and fruitcakes. Why do I not tell it all to you instead, Mrs. Beauclerk, and give her a respite?"

"Yes!" his mother cried. "I want to hear every detail." She turned to Vander, her eyes aflame. "Well, Vander?"

He blinked at his mother, uncomprehending. "Well, what?"

"Aren't you going to ask Letty to dance?" she hissed.

Dear God. Could his mother possibly be any more embarrassing?

But... it happened that he did want to speak with Letty.

Only so they could discuss the next young lady to whom he would like to be introduced. Dancing with Letty would give them the chance to converse. It was the pragmatic thing to do. Nothing more.

Horse shit, whispered a little voice in the back of his head.

He quashed that voice and bowed to Letty. "Lady Leticia, may I have the honor?"

"O-of course," she sputtered, her cheeks turning a becoming shade of pink.

Then, they were crossing the ballroom together, his mother and Emily having scurried away, leaving them alone.

Vander had been to Lady Waldegrave's house several times before, but he had never noticed how beautiful her ballroom was. Tonight, its Wedgewood-blue walls were complemented by urns overflowing with white carnations. The parquet floor seemed to sparkle in the light of the six crystal chandeliers glinting overhead.

And Letty, smiling shyly up at him, looked lovely in a dress of jonquil yellow silk with red satin roses ringing the hem.

Funny—he'd always thought he hated balls. Yet, here he was, happier than he'd been in weeks.

Months, that little voice whispered. *Quite possibly years.*

The dance was a Scotch reel, which meant they were too busy skipping and kicking and hopping from foot to foot to accomplish any conversation. Three furious minutes later, the dance ended, and they were both breathing hard.

Vander looped his arm through Letty's and started toward the French doors that led out onto the balcony. "I could use some air after that."

"Me, too." Letty pressed her free hand to her chest. "Could we get some punch first?"

Without breaking stride, Vander snagged two glasses of champagne from the tray of a passing footman, carrying them in one hand. "I believe we can do better than punch."

She shook her head, but she was smiling. "You're a bad influence, you know."

"Of course, I am." They stepped out onto the balcony, and Vander led her over to a spot along the stone balustrade. "But you could use a bad influence in your life." He handed her a glass. "Cheers."

"Cheers." Letty clinked her glass against his, then hummed with pleasure as she took her first sip.

The sensual sound went straight to his groin. Suddenly he couldn't tear his eyes from the neckline of her dress. It was wide, baring a hint of shoulder, and skimmed across the upper swells of her breasts, giving a tantalizing hint of the curves concealed by her corsetry.

"So," Letty said, resting her glass upon the balustrade, "what did you think of Miss Seymour?"

Miss Seymour? Who the hell was Miss Seymour?

Then he remembered—Miss Seymour, the woman he had

met that very afternoon. The one he had ostensibly brought Letty out onto this balcony to discuss.

Wait... there was no ostensibly about it. The entire reason he was here was to discuss Miss Seymour and his next prospective bride. He hadn't come out here to do... other things.

Horse shit, that irritating little voice whispered again.

Vander cleared his throat. "Although she was a significant improvement compared to Miss Peabody, I'm afraid we would not suit."

"No?" He would have expected Letty to look irked that he had rejected yet another of her candidates, especially as, he had to admit, Miss Seymour had met his requirements quite admirably.

Instead, she looked... relieved.

"What was the matter this time?" Letty asked.

"We had nothing in common. The topics in which she held an interest I found a bit dull, and vice versa. And what was worse, I made a remark that was slightly—and I mean *slightly*—suggestive, and she looked to be on the verge of swooning."

Letty laughed. When she glanced up at him, her eyes were twinkling with mischief. "And goodness knows, your future bride must possess a high tolerance for innuendo."

"Precisely. A leopard cannot change its spots. I'm not going to transform into some choirboy the moment I take my vows."

"Fair enough. So, let's see, you want someone who is beautiful, intelligent, and, let us say, sophisticated." She turned toward the darkened gardens, leaning against the rail. "My task grows more difficult by the day."

Vander took up a place on the balustrade next to her. "Not so difficult, surely. I really just want someone I can talk to." He nudged her with his shoulder. "You know, the way I can talk to you."

Come on, Vander, that vexing little voice whispered. *You were third wrangler. You're not an idiot. If the woman you can talk to is Letty, the woman whose company you enjoy is Letty, and the woman whose bosom you can't stop staring at is Letty, then the woman you should marry is—*

He ruthlessly quashed that thought. Because he absolutely could not marry Letty! She deserved someone better than him. And David. He couldn't forget about David.

Just about everything in his life was going to hell right now. If he went and ruined his friendship with David by dangling after his little sister, he wouldn't have anything left.

Beside him, Letty's shoulder stiffened. "Someone you can talk to as you can talk to me, just not me. I understand you perfectly." She said it lightly, but her cheerfulness sounded forced. She looked at him at last, and her smile did not reach her eyes. "We're going to Vauxhall tomorrow night. If you will consent to join us, I'll see if I can arrange your next introduction."

"That would be wonderful. Thank you." Vander cleared his throat. He hadn't meant to steer the conversation into such awkward territory. He sought a change of subject. "So, how are things with your suitors? Have you taken my advice?"

Letty's cheeks went scarlet, and she jerked her gaze back to the gardens below. "Y-your advice?" she stammered. "You mean, about kissing them again?"

Well, shit. So much for steering the conversation out of awkward territory.

Vander found that he wasn't much in the mood to discuss Letty kissing Strickleton or Throckmorton, but it was too late to change course. "Er... yes. Did you find a chance to kiss Strickleton, or—"

"At the *British Museum*?" Letty's laugh was slightly wild. "What was I supposed to do, pull him inside one of the sarcophaguses?"

That startled a chuckle out of him. "Well, I'm sure someone must've done it before."

"I highly doubt it," Letty muttered. "Kissing someone inside a sarcophagus sounds like the plot of the world's most ridiculous novel. But, to answer your question, no, an opportunity did not present itself for me to kiss Mr. Strickleton—"

Good, growled the voice in his head.

"—but I took your advice with regards to Lord Throckmorton this very evening," she said in a rush, cheeks aflame.

What the hell? He could admit—grudgingly—that Strickleton had a certain appeal. But why the hell would Letty want to kiss a stuffy old man like Throckmorton?

Because those are the choices she has. We've been through this, Vander. Try to keep up.

He gripped the balustrade with white knuckles. "And how was it?" he asked, his voice strangled.

Letty kept her gaze fixed upon the gardens. "Suffice to say, the experience did not improve with repetition."

Good.

No. No, it wasn't good. Letty might very well spend the rest of her life kissing Throckmorton. Did he want her to be miserable? What kind of uncharitable churl was he?

If he was a decent fellow, he would help her.

And there was only one way he could think of to help her.

Vander glanced around and found the balcony deserted. Grabbing Letty's hand, he hurried toward the stone steps that led down into the garden.

"Vander?" Her voice was breathless. "Wh-what are you doing?"

He towed her down a graveled path toward an arched door. "The problem is, if you've never had a proper kiss yourself, you have little hope of coaxing either of your suitors into doing better."

They passed through the door into a walled garden. It was quiet back here, the sounds of the ball diminishing to a distant thrum. The path led beneath a series of arched trellises upon which red roses were just starting to bloom. More flowers in yellow and blue filled the beds lining the path.

Letty tugged him to a halt beneath one of the trellises. "What, exactly, are you suggesting?"

One of his hands came up, brushing the fringe back from her forehead and curling behind her ear. When he spoke, his voice was pitched an octave lower than usual. "Do you not want me to?"

He could feel her pulse fluttering beneath his fingers at the place his hand had settled upon her neck.

She swallowed thickly. "I think you're right. It's the sensible thing to do."

He brought his other hand up and framed her face. "Sensible. Precisely."

That's all this was. He was kissing her because it was practical. It was the most efficient way for her to learn. He was only trying to help her.

As a friend.

Horse sh— that irksome little voice started to say.

But Vander silenced it by bringing his lips down upon Letty's.

Chapter Thirteen

L etty thought her heart might burst.

Vander was kissing her. It was actually happening. The moment she had spent an embarrassing number of hours dreaming about was finally here.

And she knew he wasn't kissing her for the usual reasons—desire, affection, love. He was doing her a favor. He was kissing her because when it came to kissing, she was inept. Which was slightly humiliating.

But in that pregnant moment when he had asked what she wanted, she hadn't hesitated. If this was her only opportunity to kiss the man she'd loved for half her life, she was going to seize it.

Vander's kiss was completely different from those she'd experienced with Bertie and Lord Throckmorton. His kiss was neither wet nor dry.

Vander's kiss was *molten*.

Not that Letty knew so much about kisses, but it didn't feel like Vander was kissing her as a favor. It felt like he really wanted her. She decided she was going to pretend it was true.

Vander sucked her bottom lip between his and she gasped.

This was all the opening he needed to caress her lips with his tongue. It felt so beautiful that her body began to tremble.

Well. That wasn't quite true. She'd already been trembling, but her body began trembling *harder*, and she began to feel light-headed to the point that she had to grab onto his shoulders for purchase. Vander wrapped his arms around her waist and pulled her flush against his chest, and *oh*—that was better. Or maybe it was worse. She couldn't seem to make up her mind.

On the one hand, it was better in that his body pressing up against hers felt delicious, but it was much, much worse for her sense of vertigo.

He was doing something wonderful with his tongue, using it to caress hers in a way that made her knees wobble, and she thought that perhaps she should try to return the favor. Her attempts felt clumsy, but Vander gave an encouraging growl, which made her feel better about them.

There was one thing she had always wanted to do, and it occurred to her that this would probably be her one and only chance to try it. So, she slid her hands up from his shoulders and threaded her fingers into his hair. And oh! It was every bit as thick and silky as it looked. She couldn't help but run her fingers through it, and he groaned as she grazed his scalp with her nails.

He tore his lips from hers, and the sound of disappointment that emerged unbidden from her lips was slightly pathetic. But her disappointment didn't last long, because Vander promptly began kissing his way across her cheek, pausing at her ear before descending to her neck. And—*merciful heavens*—that felt every bit as good as it had when he was kissing her lips! Her back arched and she made a whimpering sound, and she could feel him smile against her neck for just an instant before he continued his journey south.

As his lips were moving down, his hands were moving up. She felt his thumb graze the lower swell of her breast. Suddenly she felt overheated in the chilly night air, and her nipples were throbbing against her stays. Vander's progress had slowed, and he was pressing hot kisses into the tender skin just above the neckline of her gown. Her fingers were still tangled in his hair, and she was wondering whether he would think her a hussy if she were to press his head lower when the sound of feminine laughter drifted across the night air.

Vander's head snapped up, and they both turned toward the arched door that was the only way in or out of the walled rose garden. Now two voices were distinguishable, a man's and a woman's, as well as the crunch of footsteps upon gravel.

Someone was coming. Someone was coming, and they were trapped within the walled garden, and Letty was about to be ruined.

Moving with the swift grace of a panther, Vander scooped her up in his arms, carrying her against his chest as he plunged knee-deep into the flowerbeds. Emerging into the strip of grass on the other side, he stepped behind a trellis as he set her down, pressing her as deep into the shadows as he could. He hastily flipped up the collar on his black evening coat to hide his white shirt, then unbuttoned it. "Here," he hissed, pulling the front flaps open, "put your arms inside."

His coat was certainly less conspicuous than Letty's yellow dress, so she hastily complied. His body was warm in the cool night air, and something about their position, his forehead pressed against her temple, her fingers stroking over the silk panel on the back of his waistcoat, felt so *right*, it was all she could do not to sigh aloud.

Her face was buried in his shoulder, so she couldn't see who the man and woman were, but she heard the crunch of their footsteps upon the graveled path. "It's so beautiful," the feminine voice exclaimed.

The footsteps stopped beneath the trellis behind which they

hid. Letty could hear Vander's heartbeat thundering beneath her ear, and her pulse was flying just as fast.

"It is," the man replied. "But there's an even better spot, a gazebo." The footsteps resumed, heading back toward the arched door. "It's just a little farther down..."

The footsteps grew softer and the voices more muffled, until Letty was certain they had left the rose garden.

"Come," Vander whispered. "We should get you back to the party before we're discovered."

He scooped her up again and carried her through the flowerbed. They hastily straightened their clothing, then jogged hand-in-hand along the graveled path to the foot of the stone steps.

"Stay here," Vander whispered, then hurried up the stairs. He returned seconds later. "It's clear. We left the ballroom together, and we'll return together. If anyone asks, we've been on the balcony the whole time."

Letty nodded and accepted his arm. They climbed the steps and went through the French doors that led back into the ballroom.

She had to stop short to keep from ploughing into Lord Throckmorton.

"Lady Leticia, there you are. Your brother said you had stepped out onto the balcony with Mr. Beauclerk."

Vander's arm turned to stone beneath her hand. Letty glanced up at him and found his gaze fixed upon the far wall.

Lord Throckmorton did not seem to notice anything amiss. "I believe the next dance is mine."

He was probably right. Letty had no idea. Her interlude with Vander in the garden had wiped every other thought from her brain.

She accepted the baron's proffered arm. He turned to Vander. "Oh, and Beauclerk—Lord Trundley wanted to speak to you. He's over in the corner, talking to Lord Dormer."

Vander's eyes were darting all over the ballroom. "Oh, I... I don't have time to speak to him tonight, I have to, uh..." Straightening, he bowed over Letty's hand. "Lady Leticia, it has been a pleasure. Make my excuses to my mother, won't you?"

He spun on his heel, and Letty watched his dark head weave through the crowd and go out the ballroom doors.

Chapter Fourteen

The following morning, Vander strolled through the doors of Beauclerk Marine Casualty at half-ten.

He was sorting the stack of papers he'd brought with him when his father stormed into Vander's closet... er, office.

"Evander Beauclerk!" his father snapped. "What is the meaning of this?"

Vander peered at his father over the tops of his spectacles. "What is the meaning of what?"

"I told you to report to work at seven o'clock sharp!" his father said, jabbing his index finger against the table. "If you are to run this business, you cannot wander in whenever it suits you."

Vander rolled his eyes. "I reported to work at eight. Believe me, that was unpalatable enough." He'd only managed to wake as early as he had because he had abandoned his plans to go to Boodle's for another night at the gaming tables. He'd made it all the way to the door when he realized that his concentration was shot to pieces after his kiss with Letty. He could think of nothing but the sweet sigh she had made when his lips touched hers, how perfect she had felt in his arms, the shudder that went through him when she threaded her fingers into his hair...

"I don't know how you can say that with a straight face!" his father snapped, shattering Vander's vision of the moonlit garden and recalling him to his closet. "You *just* walked in. I *saw* you!"

Vander returned to the papers he'd been examining before his father's dramatic entrance. "True. But you will note that I said I reported to *work*. Not that I reported to this dank cell of a room."

His father crossed his arms. "And where exactly have you been?"

Vander smirked because he knew he was about to win. "Gole's Depot."

His father's eyes bugged out behind his spectacles. "G-Gole's Depot?" Gole's Depot was a boardinghouse the East India Company contracted with to provide lodging for Indian sailors over the winter before ships began hiring them for the voyages back to India that were made in the spring. It was just off Ratcliffe Highway—not the sort of neighborhood Vander usually frequented. "What on earth were *you* doing at Gole's Depot?"

"Speaking to the lascars who sailed with the *Windermere*." His papers finally in order, Vander smacked the stack against his palm. "I am happy to report that a few of them were still there. Would you like to know what cargo she had in her hold when she sailed out of Bombay?"

His father was already pulling out a plain wooden chair. "*Yes.*"

"There were no spices. Just silks, shawls, and muslin—precisely the products that arrived safe and sound in London."

His father frowned. "How can they know for sure?"

"You don't even need to open a trunk full of cinnamon, or anise, or turmeric, to know what's inside. You can smell it from twenty feet away."

His father considered for a moment. "That's likely true."

"They also saw no evidence of any cargo being dumped overboard, or any empty space in the hold where those casks had once been stacked."

"Which is suspicious but not necessarily conclusive. Just

because they didn't see it doesn't prove it didn't happen. That's the trouble—it's impossible to prove a negative."

Vander took off his spectacles and tapped them on the table. "Still, the evidence is damning. If you decide to quote the policy again, I would double their rates. At least."

His father's nostrils flared. "I don't intend to quote it at all. I hope you will excuse my strong language, but this sort of behavior is absolute Tommy-rot!"

Vander struggled to keep a straight face at his father's notion of profanity. "Good. If they're capable of this, God knows what else they might try. Something occurred to me while I was down at Gole's Depot—I managed well enough today as most of the men spoke Persian, and we found someone to act as translator for those who did not. But if you're going to insure the route to India, you should have a clerk on staff who speaks both Persian and Hindustani."

"You're probably right." His father shook his head. "I'm still having difficulty picturing *you* at Gole's Depot."

Vander grinned. "I did stand out a bit." This was a rather spectacular understatement. When he walked in, the sailors had gawked at him in his Hoby boots and exquisitely tailored charcoal grey coat as if he were the giraffe at the Tower menagerie. But after he handed out some cigars and explained why he was there—in Persian—they'd warmed to him quickly enough.

"I'll find someone for the clerk position," Vander offered. It wasn't remotely unusual for officers of the East India Company to father children with Indian women during their years abroad, and many of those children accompanied their fathers to Britain once their tenure with the Company concluded. What was more unusual was for those British fathers to legally marry the mothers of those children. It wasn't always the way it happened, but for every man like Vander, William Kirkpatrick, or the Earl of Darrow, who were legitimate, rich, and accepted in the highest circles of society, there were several who were stuck on the fringes because their father had neglected to grace his children with his last name.

Vander could think of a dozen such men who would almost certainly be thrilled by the prospect of a respectable job at Beauclerk Marine Casualty.

His father's gaze was fixed upon the table, a tight frown upon his face.

"What's wrong, Father?"

His father shifted in his seat. "It just struck me that, although my risk analysis skills are strong, Beauclerk Marine Casualty is at something of a disadvantage because I have difficulty obtaining extraneous information of this nature."

Vander blinked at his father. "You mean you're not good at... leaving the office and talking to people?"

His father burst from his chair and began pacing the narrow width of the closet. "It sounds ridiculous when you put it like that. But yes. We do not all possess your easy nature, Evander, your ability to get people to open up to you, whether they are lascars or lords." He wrung his hands in front of his heart. "I feel like they know all the latest gossip over at Lloyds, and it factors into their decisions. It puts me at a disadvantage."

Vander leaned back in his chair. "Lloyd's started out as a coffee house. The sort of place where people like to gather." Although the coffee house had closed when they moved to the Royal Exchange, Lloyd's still had the feel of a gentlemen's club, where deals were made and information changed hands.

His father shook his head. "Well, we don't have a coffee house."

An idea was forming in Vander's head. "We could, though," he muttered.

Why not? They needed to move the offices out of this abysmal hovel, anyway.

What if they chose a building large enough that they could set up a coffee house on the ground floor? One that catered to ship captains, so that all the latest gossip would be changing hands right beneath their noses...

His father spun on his heel. "What was that, Evander?"

"Nothing." Better not to mention it until he had the perfect plan. An idea so flawless even his father wouldn't be able to say no. "So, what do you want me to look at today?"

His father gestured to a dispiritingly high stack of policies and began briefing Vander on what he could expect to find.

"I'll get through as many of them as I can before four o'clock," Vander said.

His father reared back, scandalized. "You don't mean to leave at *four*?"

"I do. I'm supposed to meet the Daughtrys at Vauxhall. Letty is introducing me to another potential bride." His father started to speak, and Vander cut him off. "And it would be better for us both if you could put any ideas about me working the kind of hours that you maintain out of your head. I'm not going to work twelve-hour days. I want to have a life outside of this office."

His father shook his head. "You don't understand how much work it takes to keep this place running."

The more Vander saw, the more he suspected that half of his father's tasks could be delegated. But again, it was better not to say as much before he had a well-formed plan. "That's what I'm able to offer."

"Fine," his father grumbled, heading for the door. "See how much you're able to get through."

Rubbing his brow, Vander put his spectacles back on and tried to focus on the policies.

But his thoughts kept drifting to Letty.

Chapter Fifteen

Later that afternoon, Vander was preparing to depart for Vauxhall when there was a knock at the door of his bachelor apartments.

His valet, Richards, went to answer. "Lord Trundley is here to see you, sir."

Shit. What was David doing here? To be sure, David used to drop by all the time, but that was before he'd started courting Emily. These days it was all Vander could do to get David to meet him at White's for a drink.

If he'd bothered to come here, it could only mean one thing— he had seen Vander and Letty step out onto the balcony, and he knew exactly what they'd been up to in the gardens.

Well, if he was going to get punched in the face, he probably deserved it. A scoundrel like him had no business sniffing around Letty.

He just hoped this wouldn't be the end of his friendship with David.

Vander eyed his friend warily as he stepped into the room. But David had a broad grin on his face. "Vander! I've been trying to track you down all day. I guess Throckmorton didn't give you my message last night."

"Oh, er—"

Fortunately, David ploughed on without waiting for a response. "Then this morning, I sent a note to see if you could meet me at White's. Imagine my surprise when the response came back from Richards that you were at Beauclerk Marine Casualty."

"That's right. My father wants me to start learning the business."

"That's grand." David glanced around. "Aren't you going to ask me to sit down?"

"Of—of course." Vander gestured hastily to the sofa. "Let me get you something."

At the sideboard, he made a show of considering the half-dozen bottles. But what he really wanted was a moment to compose himself. David seemed... remarkably normal. He gave no indication of being on the cusp of punching Vander in the face.

Although appearances could be deceiving...

Vander cleared his throat. "Fancy a glass of Quinta do Noval? I've the Waterloo Vintage."

David responded with a low whistle. "'Course I do. You always have the good stuff."

Vander poured two glasses and handed one to David before taking the chair next to the sofa.

"Cheers, mate," David said, clinking his glass against Vander's. They both drank, and David settled back against the cushions. "So, how've you been?"

They chatted for a few minutes, about how Vander's life had changed since his father's ultimatum. "Letty's actually helping me search for some woman who would be willing to have me. In fact, I'm supposed to meet your family at Vauxhall in an hour," he said apologetically.

David drained his glass. "I know all about it. I'm going too, of course. I thought we could share a wherry across the river, seeing as we haven't caught up in a while."

"Great. I'd like that." Vander's voice didn't sound very enthusiastic to his own ears, but he tried to look pleased at the prospect. "Shall we, then?"

In the hackney carriage on the way to Westminster, David asked Vander how everything was going at his father's insurance office.

"I'm leading the company in bold new directions," Vander noted. "Under my guidance, Beauclerk Marine Casualty is about to corner the market for Peruvian bird shit."

David barked out a laugh. "Quit bamming me."

"I'm dead serious."

Vander told David about his days at the insurance office. In turn, David told Vander about his budding campaign for Parliament. "I'm actually leaving first thing in the morning. I'll be canvassing for votes over in Colchester. I'll be back by Tuesday, though. Got to be there for Lady Sunderland's ball. That's when Letty's announcing which of her suitors she's going to accept."

"That's on Tuesday?" Vander shook his head. "I didn't realize it was so soon."

David peered at him across the carriage. "Which of them do you think she should choose?"

Vander slouched down against the squabs, not bothering to conceal his lack of enthusiasm. "I don't know. If I'm being honest, I can't really picture her with either of them."

David muttered something that might have been, "If only she had another option."

Vander gave his friend a sharp look. "What was that?"

Abruptly, David was all smiles. "Nothing, old man. Nothing at all. So, done any boxing recently?"

They chattered about their usual topics for the remainder of the carriage ride, and Vander began to relax. David seemed like his usual self. Maybe he hadn't seen him leave the ballroom with his little sister. Maybe he wasn't going to strangle him and throw his body in the Thames.

It wasn't until the wherry had pushed off from the dock, when Vander had no hope of escape, that David said, "I saw you dancing with Letty last night."

His eyes shot to David's, wary. "What of it?"

David's voice was careful. "And then you two stepped out onto the balcony."

Vander had the rear-facing seat, meaning he had a view of the docks receding behind them. If he jumped out now, he could swim the distance. It wouldn't be easy, as he was wearing boots, but he could manage it.

Of course, failing to die of drowning meant he would have a painful, lingering death from whatever diseases he would catch from the Thames.

"Well?" David was looking at him, his expression curiously blank.

"It was a Scotch reel, you know," Vander said in a rush. "Very fast. So we were both a bit winded, and the ballroom was so crowded. Crowded and loud. And I needed to talk to her. About Miss Seymour, the woman she'd introduced me to that afternoon at the British Museum. It's the reason I was there—so we'd have a chance to talk. So, that's why I took her out on the balcony. So we'd have a place where we—"

"Could talk," David said with him in unison. "So, that's the only reason you took her out on the balcony?"

"Of course!" Vander tried to chuckle. It came out sounding like his father's laugh, high-pitched and nervous. "Come on, David. You don't think *me* and... and *Letty*?"

David tilted his head. "No?"

"Absolutely not," Vander hastened to reassure him.

"Oh." David gazed out at the river. After a moment, he nodded, then grinned at Vander. "Well, if this Miss Seymour didn't work out, you'd better get cracking. You've only got, what, three weeks to find the future Mrs. Beauclerk?"

"Twenty-five days," Vander retorted. "But who's counting?"

They both laughed, and the conversation drifted to other subjects. David did not punch Vander in the face, nor was he forced to leap into the Thames. And by the time the wherry pulled up to the Vauxhall docks, the ease with which he usually conversed with his best friend had returned.

Almost.

Chapter Sixteen

L etty peered around the column of the Daughtry family's supper box to observe Vander's approach. David had announced that he would collect Vander and meet them there, and surely enough, there they were, strolling up the path with their heads bent together, laughing at some joke understood only by the two of them.

Vander wore stone grey breeches and a black tailcoat. Truly, no one looked half so handsome in black evening wear as Vander, with his glossy black hair and golden skin perfectly offset by his snow-white linen...

Beneath the table, Emily squeezed her hand, a gesture Letty gratefully returned. Only Emily knew how hard this was, having to match Vander with another woman.

Especially when the woman she was to introduce him to was as exquisite as Beatrice Haddington Barnet. Letty didn't know why she hadn't thought of Mrs. Barnet immediately. She was perfect for Vander in every way. Sophisticated. Clever. In possession of a fine wit.

She was a widow, but she was a young, beautiful widow with brown hair and sparkling green eyes. She was just jaded enough for it to be fashionable rather than tiresome, and she had a worldly air about her Letty was sure Vander would find appealing. There was nothing he could find objectionable about Mrs. Barnet. Absolutely nothing.

Letty felt a horrible foreboding that tonight, Vander would be spending the evening with his future bride. And she would be the one to make it possible.

Emily squeezed her hand again as David and Vander approached the table. They were the last to arrive. The supper box was enclosed by wooden walls on three sides and topped with a roof to keep out the frequently inclement English weather. A plain wooden bench lined each of the walls. Letty's parents were seated to her left, she and Emily were squeezed in along the supper box's back wall, and they had left the right bench open for David and Vander.

"Switch places with me, Letty," were the first words out of David's mouth. "I want to sit next to Emily."

"And good evening to you, too, brother," Letty muttered, sliding around the table.

She made it to the opening and started to stand, but her skirt must've snagged on something because she stumbled as she attempted to rise. David was making eyes with Emily and didn't even notice.

But Vander surged forward and caught her beneath the arms before she could fall face first in the dirt.

"Sorry, Letty," David said cheerfully. "That was my fault. I seem to have trod upon your hem."

Vander swiftly removed his hands from the more intimate areas of her anatomy—more's the pity—but offered her his hand before she could sway. "Are you all right?" he murmured, brown eyes creased with concern.

"I'm fine." Other than the fact that she'd just made a cake of herself in front of the man she'd been in love with for most of her life. "Thanks to you."

"Good." Vander placed his other hand on the small of her back to help her back onto the bench, and Letty shuddered.

Emily was giving David a reproachful look. David grinned, not seeming to notice. "So, how many chickens do you think we'll have to order to get an entire bite?"

He was referring to the portions at Vauxhall, which were notoriously small. While her family began debating what to order, Letty nudged Vander with her elbow. "I think you'll like the woman I've arranged for you to meet tonight," she whispered.

Vander dropped his voice low. "David said earlier that the ball at which you'll have to choose between your suitors is on Tuesday. Is that true?"

"It is. Regarding the woman to whom I'll be introducing you —her name is Beatrice Haddington Barnet, and—"

"I don't want to talk about Beatrice Haddington... whoever she is," Vander muttered.

Letty gave an annoyed huff. "I presumed that you might have *some* interest in her, which is why I went to the trouble to arrange an introduction."

Vander gave her a baleful look. "That's not what I meant. Of course, I'm grateful for your help. But I've got until the end of the month. You've only got three more days! Are you any closer to figuring out who you're going to accept?"

Letty squeezed her eyes shut. "I am not."

She could feel his breath hot on her ear as he whispered, "We've got to do something."

She gave him a sideways look. "What, exactly, are we going to do?"

"Well, for starters, we can—"

"What are you two talking about?" They both jumped at the sound of David's question.

"Nothing!" they replied in startled unison.

David grinned lazily. "It certainly sounds like nothing."

The waiter appeared, and Letty's father ordered a variety of dishes.

Vander took advantage of the distraction to lean in to Letty's ear. "If you've only got three days, it is imperative that you determine which of them will be more tolerable."

Letty sighed. "I'm not sure it matters. At this point, I doubt I'm going to find marital bliss with either of them. Maybe the best thing is for me to accept that and look elsewhere for my personal happiness."

Vander was studying her in a way that made her want to look away. "Is that what you want?" he whispered.

She gave a startled laugh. "Of course not."

His brown eyes bore into hers. "What do you want?"

She looked away then, afraid that he would see the answer in her eyes. *You, Vander. Always you.*

"Nothing I'm likely to get in the next three days," she finally answered, still not meeting his eye.

From across the table, her father boomed, "And bring us one of those cheesecakes. That should get us started."

She and Vander jerked guiltily apart. The waiter was heading toward the kitchens, but Vander grabbed his sleeve before he could retreat. "We'd also like a bottle of champagne," he murmured. "Unless Lord Baldridge ordered one already?"

"He did not, Mr. Beauclerk."

"Then bring us one. And I'll take the bill," Vander whispered.

The waiter looked surprised. "For the champagne, sir?"

"For everything," Vander said firmly.

"Yes, sir," the waiter said, departing with a bow.

Letty poked him in the arm. "My father won't like that."

"If you'll keep your voice down, it is my hope that he won't even notice."

"He might not, but it's the principle of the—"

"So, Vander," her father said in his booming voice. "David tells me you're training to take over your father's business."

Vander sprang to attention. "That is correct, my lord."

The conversation turned in other directions. Then the food arrived, and Vander filled Letty's glass with champagne before her mother could object. When her mother frowned, he turned to her at once. "May I fill your glass, Lady Baldridge?"

"Oh, er..." She shifted uncomfortably in her seat, but Vander's smile was so charming, she apparently didn't have the heart to chastise him. "That would be lovely."

Letty ate Vauxhall's famous ham, sliced so thinly it bore more resemblance to a spiderweb than a piece of meat, and chickens so small a whole bird fit in the palm of her hand. At least there was bread and butter enough to fill her stomach. They spoke of Vander's work at his father's company and David's upcoming trip to Colchester to canvass for votes.

"I thought your father and I would accompany him as far as Chelmsford," Letty's mother said. "It will give me a chance to drop in and visit my Aunt Agatha. Won't you come with us, Letty?"

She hastily set down her wineglass. "I'd best stay in Town, don't you think? What with Lady Sunderland's ball looming on the horizon."

Her mother's lips tightened. "Then you still haven't made up your mind?"

"No. I'll do so by Tuesday. I'm just trying to make the most informed decision I can."

Her mother was shaking her head. "It should be the easiest decision you'll ever make."

"Well, it's not," Letty muttered under her breath. Beneath the table, Vander nudged her with his knee. When she looked up, his eyes were sympathetic.

"My mother can act as her chaperone," Emily offered. "There's a rout at Mrs. Ridley's house tomorrow, and Lady Napier is hosting a Venetian breakfast on Monday. Lord Throckmorton, Mr. Strickleton, or both are likely to be in attendance. I know Mama won't mind."

"Thank you, Emily," Letty said.

"That's very kind, Emily," Letty's mother said. "Thank you."

By then the sky had darkened to midnight blue and the first stars were starting to glint through the trees. Around the grove, Vauxhall's waiters were setting down their trays and taking up positions along the strings of lamps hanging overhead.

"The lamp lighting! It's about to begin!" Emily exclaimed. She poked David in the shoulder. "Let me up! Let me up! I can't see a thing from in here."

Vander and Letty slid out of the supper box so Emily and David could make their own way out. Even Letty's parents, who had probably visited Vauxhall a hundred times, stood and strode onto the broad gravel path to watch the show.

On cue, tiny sparks broke out all around the Grove, like fireflies. The sparks turned to trails of golden light as they raced up carefully positioned wicks until each one reached its destination: glass lamps of red and yellow, green and blue. Oohs and aahs went up from the crowd as thousands of lamps sparked to life throughout the garden until it felt like being inside of a kaleidoscope. Within two minutes, the lighting was accomplished, and a scattering of cheers and applause broke out from a few of the surrounding supper boxes.

Beside her, Vander grinned. "That never gets old."

"No," Letty agreed. "No, it doesn't."

"David and I are going to go watch the Cascade," Emily announced.

"Oh, that's right!" Letty turned to Vander. "That's where we're to meet with Mrs. Barnet."

She could just make out Vander's groan, barely audible over the crowd surrounding them, which was still exclaiming over the colorful lamps.

He offered Letty his arm. "Shall we, then?"

103

"David," Letty's mother ordered, "you're to keep a close eye on your sister."

David cast his eyes heavenward. "Yes, Mother."

They trailed after Emily and David. It felt so nice, wandering the paths on Vander's arm, enjoying the cool night air and the rainbow of colors glinting in the trees overhead. It struck Letty that she would've been perfectly content, were it not for the knowledge that her idyll with Vander would be ending in a few short minutes.

They came into the little clearing that housed the Cascade. The Cascade was one of the signature attractions of Vauxhall. At first glance, it looked like a simple panorama of a pretty country scene with a river and a mill. But it had some clever mechanized features, such as a belt that conveyed shiny slivers of metal round and round to give the illusion that the river was running. The mill's wheel also turned. The automation was turned on promptly at nine o'clock each night and would run for fifteen minutes. It was now ten minutes until nine, and a crowd was starting to gather.

Across the clearing, Letty spotted Mrs. Barnet. "That's her," she whispered. "Beatrice Haddington Barnet. She's standing a little ways off from the crowd, next to that elm tree. She's wearing a rust-colored gown with a gold spencer."

Letty's heart squeezed, because Mrs. Barnet looked so beautiful standing by that elm tree in the lamplight, beautiful and forlorn, and it was impossible to imagine that Vander would not be moved by her loveliness.

"Hmm," Vander grunted. "Let's get it over with, I suppose."

Letty gave him a strange look, then shook herself. A significant crowd was forming in the meadow, and she'd already lost sight of Mrs. Barnet. Vander probably hadn't spotted her. That was the only explanation for his lack of enthusiasm.

She tugged his arm and led him to the elm tree, then forced the brittle smile she'd practiced so much over the past week to her lips. "Mrs. Barnet, it's so lovely to see you. May I present Mr. Evander Beauclerk? Mr. Beauclerk, Mrs. Beatrice Haddington Barnet."

Vander made a perfunctory bow over her hand. "Mrs. Barnet. A pleasure."

Mrs. Barnet swept into an elegant curtsey. "Likewise, Mr. Beauclerk."

Vander gestured to the Cascade. "Would you like to stay and watch the Cascade? We may have a better vantage point from—"

"Letty! There you are!" Vander was cut off by Bertie Strickleton, who came bounding into the clearing.

Vander's gaze snapped to Letty. "What's he doing here?" he hissed.

Before she could respond, Bertie burst into their group. "Sorry I'm late. I know we were supposed to meet at the lamp lighting. But you'll never guess who I ran into at White's this afternoon!"

"Was it Figgy?" Letty asked with a solemnity she did not feel.

"No-ho!" Bertie punctuated this by swinging his index finger. "Good guess, though. It was Cheggers!"

"Good old Cheggers," Letty murmured.

"Good old Cheggers, indeed!" Bertie offered her his arm. "Well, he wanted to go to Manton's to shoot, so we swung by my apartments to get my dueling pistols, and then..."

Letty fixed a bland smile upon her lips as she settled in for another evening of Bertie's inane chatter.

"Say, now," Bertie said, "you don't want to watch the Cascade, do you? I'm sick to death of the thing. I must've seen it six times—no, seven. Or is it eight?"

In truth, Letty had wanted to see the Cascade. She, too, had seen it a few times, but not so many that it was no longer diverting. But she bowed her head. "That's fine, Bertie. We can go somewhere else if you like."

"Capital, capital." Bertie was already leading her away.

"Hang on," Vander said. "Where's David?"

Letty glanced around the clearing. Unsurprisingly, David and Emily were nowhere to be seen. "I imagine he's taken Emily off so they can be alone."

"But you need a chaperone," Vander protested.

Letty almost snorted. How dearly she wished an evening of intrigue and romance awaited her in the dark walks.

To be sure, Bertie might subject her to a sloppy kiss or two. But she was fairly certain she would spend the majority of the night listening to him describe his day in wearisome detail.

She gave Vander a wry smile. "Look who's suddenly concerned about propriety. Don't worry. I promise to stay out of trouble."

Vander frowned. "Letty, wait."

She didn't want to wait, didn't want to give him the chance to suggest the four of them make up their own party. The only thing worse than an evening of Bertie's company would be watching the man she pined after fall head over heels in love with Beatrice Haddington Barnet.

So, she waved over her shoulder and let Bertie lead her down the path.

He tilted his head toward hers. "As I was saying, me and Cheggers headed off to Manton's, and you'll never guess who we met there..."

Allowing her attention to drift, Letty glanced over her shoulder to nod farewell to Vander and Mrs. Barnet.

She found Vander staring back at her, his face as dark as a thundercloud.

She was left with that to ponder as Bertie led her off into the night.

Chapter Seventeen

V ander stared after Letty and Strickleton's retreating
forms, thunderstruck.

He didn't know why it hadn't occurred to him that
she would be meeting with one of her suitors tonight. That was
her entire goal for the next three days—to spend as much time in
their company as possible, so she could decide which one to
marry.

It bothered him that it was Strickleton. Throckmorton was
old and dull, and they'd established last night that he was a hope-
lessly bad kisser. Not that he particularly *liked* the idea of Letty
having a tete-a-tete with Throckmorton.

But he could *tolerate* it. Whereas Strickleton? Young, handsome, charming, effervescent Bertie Strickleton?

Vander found that he could not stand the idea of her strolling
the romantic lamplit paths with Bertie Strickleton. And even
worse than the lamplit paths was the thought of them venturing
into the dark walks toward the back of the garden, where couples
went to kiss... and more.

Vander was *quite* familiar with those dark walks. He knew

what sorts of debauchery one got up to in the dark walks, as he'd taken advantage of them on more than one occasion.

But the thought of Letty and Strickleton making use of them...

His vision swam in an angry red haze.

"Mr. Beauclerk? Mr. Beauclerk?"

He snapped his attention back to the woman he was ostensibly supposed to be escorting tonight. "Mrs. Barret. I beg your pardon."

"It's Mrs. *Barnet*," she noted.

"Mrs. Barnet," he amended, bowing. "A thousand apologies."

She regarded him with an amused smile. "That's quite all right. I do wish to forewarn you, however"—she dropped her voice to a murmur—"Letty was so dear when she asked if she could introduce us tonight that I didn't have the heart to tell her no. But I have no intention of marrying again."

"That's fine," Vander said, returning his gaze to Letty and Strickleton. Just as he had feared, they were heading toward the back of the gardens...

"Then there is the fact that you are a scoundrel of such repute that you were featured in the *Rake Review*." She gave a humorless laugh. "I know that many women find rakish types terribly dashing. But my former husband was a rake, you see, and I have had more than my fill of them."

"Quite understandable," Vander said, craning his neck to track Letty and Strickleton's progress.

They had just reached the edge of the grove. A few more steps and they would be out of his sight.

He turned to his companion. "Do you wish to stay and watch the Cascade?"

One corner of her mouth twisted up. "I've seen it before if you would prefer to go somewhere else."

"If you don't mind," he said, smoothly taking her arm and

striding after Letty. "There are some very nice sights in this direction."

"Is that so?" she asked, giving him an arch look. "Here I had formed the impression that most of the attractions were toward the front of the garden."

"That is true, generally speaking, but there are the... the..." He combed his mind for anything of interest this far back in the gardens, other than Letty's retreating form. "The trees," he finally said. "There are some lovely trees."

"So, we will be looking at trees. In the dark," she added.

"Er..." Letty and Strickleton had reached a crossing. He needed to hurry or else he would lose sight of her.

"The lamps!" he said, recalling that she was still waiting for an answer. "Some of the best, most colorful lamps are back this way."

"Colorful lamps. In the dark walks. How fascinating."

Speaking of the dark walks, Letty and Strickleton had turned left, meaning that was directly where they were headed. Vander quickened his pace.

"So, Mr. Beauclerk," his companion ventured, "I understand that you enjoy boxing."

"Yes," Vander replied. His stomach was twisting into a knot at the thought of Letty getting up to... well, the things one got up to in the dark walks... with *Bertie Strickleton*...

"And what is it that you enjoy about boxing?"

"Um..." Vander craned his neck, struggling to keep Letty within his sight. "Mostly, you know. The boxing."

"And here I'd heard you were a scintillating conversationalist," she muttered.

Vander should probably apologize, but Letty and Strickleton had just rounded a corner, meaning that she was out of his sight. He quickened his strides, a clawing sort of desperation rising in his chest.

"Mr. Beauclerk!" His companion tugged him to a halt. "Are you even attending?"

He shook his head to clear it. "I apologize, Mrs. Barnard—"

"Barnet."

"Mrs. Barnet," he hastily amended. He fought the urge to stare down the path where Letty had disappeared. "I seem to be a bit distracted this evening."

She peered up at him, brow wrinkled. "You, Mr. Beauclerk, are not at all what I was expecting. Come"—she pulled him forward, following in Letty and Strickleton's footsteps—"let's look for those lamps of yours."

When they reached the crossing, Mrs. Barnet unerringly pulled him in the direction Letty and Strickleton had gone. He could just make them out some fifty yards away, and Vander breathed a sigh of relief.

That sigh turned into a growl in the next instant when Strickleton bent his head to kiss her hand—the *palm* of her hand...

The sound of feminine laughter pierced his angry red haze. He glanced at Mrs. Barnet, wary.

"Are you truly one of London's most notorious rakehells? Because you're doing a remarkable impression of a lovesick schoolboy."

Damn. He'd been caught. But although Mrs. Barnet was laughing at him, there was sympathy in her eyes.

Vander sighed. "Perhaps a bit of both."

She tutted, but not unkindly. "You've got it bad, don't you?"

He cleared his throat. "So it would seem."

"Why not just tell her?"

Vander shook his head. "It's like you said—I've got this terrible reputation. Which is deserved," he hastened to add. He ignored the pang in his chest as Strickleton reached out to tuck a lock of hair behind Letty's ear. "But Letty deserves better than the likes of me. She deserves someone like Bertie Strickleton."

Seizing his arm, Mrs. Barnet pulled him forward. "Oh, no, she doesn't. Bertie Strickleton is a dead bore."

"Is he?" Vander asked, surprised. "But he's a nice sort of chap, isn't he?"

Mrs. Barnet answered with a snort. "He's affable enough, but he's also selfish and spoiled. I can tell you this much—Bertie Strickleton isn't interested in pleasing anyone but himself."

They'd covered half of the distance separating them from Letty and Strickleton. "What are you doing?" Vander hissed. "We can't just go charging up there and... and..."

"For some inexplicable reason, I've decided to help you," she whispered. "Not because I'm entirely sure about you. Lord knows, I'm not. But I like Lady Leticia, and you're bound to be better than *Bertie Strickleton*. At least you were interesting enough to get featured in the *Rake Review*. Besides, there's something delicious about the notion of one of London's most notorious rakehells being laid low by the girl next door."

Vander peered at her skeptically. "And how, exactly, are you going to help me?"

"You'll see." Her eyes filled with poison. "But if you hurt her, know that I will start the *vilest* rumors about you!"

Abruptly, her face settled into an expression that was serene and gracious. Waving a hand overhead, she called, "Lady Leticia! Oh, Lady Leticia!"

Letty and Strickleton paused and turned.

Mrs. Barnet rushed up to them. "Would you happen to have a pin? I just noticed a tear in my hem, and I fear it will fray to pieces if I don't see to it right away."

"Oh, of course," Letty said, opening her reticule. She pulled out a short strip of paper holding a half-dozen pins. "Here, take all of these. Who knows how many you'll need."

"Thank you ever so much," Mrs. Barnet said, voice trembling with relief. She glanced back toward the front of the gardens, and her face suddenly fell. "Oh, dear. We've made so many twists and turns, I'm not entirely sure I can find my way back to the front of the gardens."

Vander almost snorted, because finding your way out of Vaux-hall was not a complex matter. The paths were straight, and the front of the garden was lit up like the Battle of Trafalgar with several thousand glowing lamps, which became scarcer and scarcer the deeper you ventured into the gardens. All one had to do to find the exit was to head toward the light.

Strickleton did not seem to question Mrs. Barnet's professed poor sense of direction. "What you want to do is head back this way, then take a left at the first crossing, then a right at the next one..."

Once he had finished, Mrs. Barnet said, "I think I have it—right at the first crossing, then left."

"It's actually left, then right," Strickleton explained.

"Oh, dear." Mrs. Barnet's face was a portrait of confusion. "I'll never remember the way." She surged forward, seizing Strickleton's arm. "But you'll show me. Won't you?"

"Er..." Strickleton frowned, gazing at Letty. "Maybe Beauclerk here could do it."

Angling her head so Strickleton couldn't see, Mrs. Barnet fixed Vander with a ferocious glower he interpreted as, *don't you dare.*

"Oh, er—I'm not entirely sure myself," Vander lied.

Mrs. Barnet was already towing Strickleton along the path. "Come. The sooner we depart, the sooner you can return. Why, I wager it won't take us even five minutes, given your superior sense of direction."

This flattery seemed to soothe whatever qualms Strickleton was harboring. "I've always been this way," he confided. "When I was but a boy of five, I could find my way from the house to the stables."

"Could you truly?" Mrs. Barnet asked as they disappeared around the first turn.

"Vander?"

He turned and found Letty gazing up at him, eyes crinkled

with confusion. She was standing beneath a lamp, its golden light falling softly upon her face, and it struck him that she was the most beautiful woman he'd ever seen.

She shook her head. "If I didn't know better, I would say that Mrs. Barnet was trying to get Bertie off on her own."

"Something like that." Vander realized that they needed to move so they would be gone by the time Strickleton returned. He hooked his arm through Letty's and started toward the back of the garden. "Come on."

"Vander!" she protested. "Where are we going? If we're not there when Bertie returns, how will he find us again?"

Vander cut his eyes to her but didn't slow his stride. "Do you really want to spend the evening with Bertie Strickleton?"

Letty seemed to deflate on his arm. "Not particularly."

"Well, then." They'd entered the farthest reaches of the gardens, but instead of turning right to head for the famous dark walks, Vander turned left. He had a particular destination in mind, one that wasn't on any map of Vauxhall, and that few people knew about. Now, where was that birch tree?

"But what about you?" Letty asked. "Don't you want to spend the evening with Mrs. Barnet?"

"Not particularly." Ah, there it was. He gestured to the thicket of trees just off the path. "Do you have sturdy shoes on?"

"They're slippers, not half boots, but I can walk in them well enough. But returning to the point—what, exactly, was wrong with my choice this time?"

Vander frowned as he led Letty into the trees. The truth was... nothing, really. Mrs. Barnet was beautiful. And, based upon their very brief acquaintance, she seemed clever, wry, and somewhat jaded with the world. A few days ago, he would have been delighted to receive an introduction to such a creature.

But Mrs. Barnet possessed one fatal flaw.

She wasn't Letty.

Mrs. Barnet had assessed his situation at a glance. He was one of the most notorious rakehells in London. Hell, he'd been featured in the bloody *Rake Review*! He'd dallied with some of the most sophisticated courtesans in Europe.

And now, his best friend's virginal sister had him twisting himself in knots.

He couldn't stop thinking about her. He craved her company. The sight of her disappearing down the path with Bertie Strickleton had gnawed a hole in his gut.

He lifted a branch and held it up so Letty could pass beneath. This far back in the gardens, the trees were thicker, and nobody had bothered to remove the underbrush. As a result, visitors rarely ventured off the path, and, in Vander's experience, this section of the gardens was almost always deserted.

Which was precisely how he wanted it.

"Vander?" Letty pulled him to a halt. "Are you going to answer my question? What, precisely, was wrong with Mrs. Barnet?"

They came around a large yew tree, and a familiar clearing opened before them. *Perfect.* He'd found it.

He turned to face her, grinning. "There wasn't anything wrong with her. I didn't pay her too much attention. I wanted to show you this."

"Show me what?" Letty reached down to tug her skirts free of some bramble. "An overgrown... *Oh!*"

Vander grinned as she noticed the swing. It was simply made, just a plain board suspended by two ropes, hanging from the branch of an oak tree. But by the light of the full moon filtering into the clearing, it took on an enchanted quality.

Letty wandered across the clearing, entranced. She reached out hesitantly and touched one of the ropes. "I've been to Vauxhall dozens of times. Why did I not know this was here?"

"Few people do. As you can see, it's not an official feature. Most of Vauxhall's accoutrements tend to be more elaborate than a plain wooden board."

The corner of her mouth turned up, drawing his gaze to her lips. "Most of Vauxhall's accoutrements are nothing more than plain wooden boards with a little paint slapped on."

He grinned. "True. But I think you'll agree that they place a great premium upon the appearance of grandeur."

"That they do. So, how did this get here?"

"I don't know. I suspect some miscreant sneaked it in and strung it up one night for their own amusement." He took hold of one of the ropes and held the swing steady. "Climb aboard. I'll push you."

She tugged one of the ropes, her face skeptical. "Why don't you go first?"

Vander shrugged. "Seems only fair."

He climbed aboard and pushed back. After a few tentative passes, he began swinging in earnest. "It's fine," he said, bouncing on the seat to make sure. "The ropes are newer than they look."

He could tell Letty wanted a turn but was trying not to look overeager. "I suppose I could give it a try."

"All right," Vander said, but instead of yielding the seat, he waited for an upswing, then caught her about the waist, pulling her into his lap.

Letty shrieked, clinging to his neck. "Evander Beauclerk! This thing had better not break."

"If it does, I'll get the worst of it." He brought his lips to her ear. "Relax."

After they made a few circuits back and forth without the ropes snapping in two, Letty did just that. She looped her arms around his neck and let her head loll against his shoulder, basking in the moonlight.

And it was perfect. The anxious moments that preceded this, when he knew with a gnawing certainty that it would be Bertie Strickleton sneaking her off to the dark walks, were forgotten. Letty was here with him—in his lap, in his arms, in his life, and it seemed to follow that all was right with the world. The cool night air was delicious on his face as he swung back and forth. It occurred to Vander that he was happy, happier than he'd been in months. He could spend all night here with Letty, doing nothing more than innocently swinging back and forth, and be perfectly content.

Although... having Letty in his lap was... tempting. In their current position, her right breast nudged his chest each time they swung forward. She smelled so good, like lily of the valley. And he could feel her bottom, which was the perfect mixture of soft and firm, pressing against his cock.

Make that his rapidly hardening cock...

Vander couldn't resist pressing a kiss against the delicate shell of her ear. She made the most wonderful sound, a startled moan, and shuddered against him. Encouraged, he began exploring her ear with his tongue.

He trailed his lips down her neck. His hands had left the ropes, all thoughts of swinging forgotten, although their momentum kept them going. He threaded his fingers into the hair at the nape of her neck, gently tipping her head back to give him better access.

He brought his lips up, trailing kisses across her jaw, but his hands down. By the time he pressed a kiss to the corner of her mouth, Letty was breathing hard, and when he brought his thumb around to graze one of her nipples through the silk of her dress, she gasped.

He claimed her lips then, and she opened for him at once, threading her fingers into his hair as she tangled her tongue with his. Vander found her artless ardor more thrilling than the practiced kiss of the most skilled courtesan. It struck him how different it was kissing Letty, compared to the many women he had dallied with over the past year. With those kisses, he had desired them physically. But tonight, he was chasing more than just a physical release. He wanted Letty to think about him as much as he'd been thinking about her the past few days. He wanted her to long for his company in the same way he longed for hers. And he wanted all of her—every smile, every whispered jest, every second of her time. Not just her body.

This kiss was real in a way that all those other kisses had not been. Oh, but he was on dangerous ground, coveting the one woman he could never have. He knew he should stop, yet he couldn't.

He traced his tongue around the rim of Letty's lips, eliciting a gasp. His hands were now discovering the delicate shape of her breasts through the silk of her dress. He could tell her nipples were exquisitely sensitive by the way she squirmed in his lap whenever he gave them the slightest brush.

He knew he shouldn't, but he couldn't resist slipping a hand inside her bodice. Her skin was as soft as rose petals, and the only thing more perfect than the feeling of it beneath his fingers was the cry of pleasure she gave in the moment his fingers found her sensitive bud.

She tore her mouth from his. "Vander," she gasped. "That feels so... so..."

He rolled her nipple lightly in his fingers, and she broke off with a cry, burying her face in his neck. Tugging her dress low on her shoulders, he eased the bodice down and lifted her breasts from the cups of her stays, exposing them to the moonlight.

She was perfect. Pert. Delicate. Gorgeous. With a groan, Vander lowered his head and sucked one of her rose-pink nipples into his mouth.

Letty gave a strangled cry, her fingernails scouring his scalp, holding his head in place. By now, she was squirming helplessly in his lap, which was having a predictable effect on his cock, which was standing up, demanding some attention.

Suddenly, Letty surprised him by hiking up her skirts and swinging one leg over so that she was straddling him. She looped her arms around his neck and leaned in to kiss him, but just as her lips were about to meet his, the swing reached the end of its arc and pushed forward, bringing the hardness of his cock into contact with the softness between her legs. There were still a few layers of wool and muslin separating them, but Vander could feel her, and, judging by the glassy look that came into her eyes, she could feel him, too.

"Vander?" she whispered. "That feels..."

The swing completed another arc, and she rocked against him again. "Vander!" she gasped.

He should have stopped things right there. A *gentleman* would have stopped, but Vander was no gentleman, and the notion of bringing Letty to climax in the moonlight suddenly seemed nigh irresistible.

He brought one hand down and started teasing her nipple again. "Do you know what's happening?"

"N-no." Her eyes were closed, and there was a trace of desperation in her voice.

"Then you've never played with it before? The little bud between your legs?"

She opened her eyes then, and they were dilated with pleasure. "What b-bud?"

"You've never touched yourself between your legs?" he asked, voice husky.

She looked startled by the suggestion. "N-no. My mother told me I wasn't allowed to touch myself there, except for washing, and even then, I had to do it as briefly as possible."

It was too sweet—he was going to be the one to give Letty her first taste of pleasure.

He pressed a kiss against her temple. "Do you want me to show you why that spot was forbidden?"

"I... I think so. I definitely don't want you to stop."

That was all he needed to hear. He started swinging in earnest, so that she was thrust against him hard, and the rest of her sentence was cut off by a desperate cry.

He positioned his hips so she was perfectly aligned against his cock. He kept swinging, kept stroking her nipples with his hands, and brought his lips down upon hers.

Letty, poor innocent, didn't stand a chance. She had no choice but to grind her hips against him, crying out when she still couldn't find the relief her body needed.

"Vander!" she gasped, tearing her lips from his. "I... I don't know what's happening..."

He kissed her throat. "It's all right. I do."

Her breath was coming in pants. "I need... something..."

He pressed a kiss against her temple. "Don't worry. I'll help you. I'm going to make it so good for you, Letty."

He hadn't meant for things to go this far, had only meant to steal a kiss or two in the moonlight, as he had done last night.

But his sweet Letty had managed to get herself painfully aroused.

He could never leave her in this state. The only gentlemanly thing to do was... the least gentlemanly thing he could possibly do.

Oh, well. He was the biggest scoundrel in London. He was obviously going to do it.

Chapter Eighteen

Letty felt like she was going to crawl out of her own skin. She had no idea what was going on, had never felt like this in her life.

But she knew she needed... something.

And she was certain Vander could give it to her.

He turned her so that her back was facing toward his front, then began drawing up her skirts. Letty shivered, but it had nothing to do with the cool night air washing over her bare legs.

She felt Vander's hands, warm upon the skin of her inner thighs, a place no one ever touched, pressing her legs open. Inch by agonizing inch, he slid them higher, toward the place that was throbbing like a heartbeat.

"Is this all right?" he murmured in her ear.

"Yes," Letty gasped. It was more than all right. She had been dreaming about a moment like this with Vander for years. Even if this was the only such moment she ever got, she would treasure it as a beautiful memory.

"Let's see what you like," he said, and then he was touching her *there*, in the spot Letty had been told she was never allowed to touch.

And it felt *glorious*.

He put one hand over her pubic bone, pressing down with the heel of his hand in a gentle grinding motion that made her squirm. He brought his other hand between her legs and proceeded to caress every inch of her flesh.

After a minute, Letty was panting. It felt... wonderful and horrible at the same time. How was that possible? She didn't know, but somehow Vander's caress felt incandescently pleasurable, *and* made her desperate for... for... she didn't even know what she was desperate for.

"Vander," she gasped. "Vander... *please*!"

He responded by unerringly bringing two fingers to a particular spot at the juncture of her thighs and gently starting to circle. Letty cried out because *this* was the thing she needed. She was certain of it. This was surely the most beautiful sensation on the face of this earth.

"Is that all right?" he whispered at her temple.

"All right?" Letty moaned. "It's more than all right. Oh, my *God*, Vander, that feels... that feels..."

She felt his vocal cords rumble as he chuckled. "It's not too much?"

"It's not," she panted. "Please, don't stop!"

He continued those teasing circles. Somehow it just kept getting better and better, until Letty knew with a strange certainty that *something* was about to happen—

Vander suddenly rose from the swing, lifting her up with him. Letty cried out in protest as he placed her back on the seat alone. "Vander! Don't stop! Please! I—I need..."

"Shh," he said, wrapping her hands around the ropes. Much to Letty's astonishment, he dropped to his knees between her thighs. "I'm going to make this so fucking good for you."

Letty was so far gone, she gave not a single word of protest as he brought his head between her legs, his lips coming all the way to the juncture of her thighs. He began stroking that magical little spot with his tongue, and *oh*! If she'd thought what he had been doing before was pleasurable, it was nothing, *nothing*, compared to the pure, unadulterated bliss he was giving her with his tongue! She cried out as her thighs cramped around the sides of his head.

Vander began massaging her on that miracle spot with the flat of his tongue, and somehow that felt even better. The pleasure he was giving her was indescribable, unbelievable. She heard herself babbling nonsense as he held her at the top of the precipice, then sent her tumbling over.

All at once, her thighs were shaking violently. She was crying out her pleasure as everything between her legs pulsed with approval. Vander somehow avoided being dislodged and kept licking her, more gently now, and it felt so beautiful, Letty could have cried.

Abruptly, the sensations became too much, and Letty's thighs tensed. Vander immediately stopped, pressing a final kiss to the inside of her thigh. He stood and lifted her from the swing, then settled with her cradled on his lap.

Letty slumped against his chest, boneless.

When her head cleared sufficiently that she was capable of speech, the words that emerged from her mouth were, "What was that?"

She felt Vander's cheek curl into a smile against her forehead. "You had a climax."

She said nothing as she was still overwhelmed. After a moment, Vander asked, "Did you like it?"

"Did I *like* it?" Of all the ridiculous questions. "It was"—she paused, combing her mind for a superlative that remotely captured the sensations Vander had just sent coursing through her — "*astonishingly* good."

Vander's chuckle thrummed in her ear. "Good."

He shifted on the swing, and she felt the same swollen hardness she had noticed earlier in the front of his trousers. Having been raised in the country, Letty had some idea what that was.

"What about you?" she asked.

Vander glanced at her, the sharp planes of his face handsome in the moonlight. "What about me?"

"Do you want me to do something for you?"

He laughed. "You don't want me to answer that."

"Of course, I do!" she protested. "Why would you say such a thing?"

His eyes were earnest in the moonlight. "Look, Letty, I don't expect you to do anything for me. It would be wildly inappropriate of me to ask it of you, even if we leave your maidenhead intact."

His words were firm, but his voice held a note of yearning. "But?" Letty prompted.

Vander snorted. "How did you know there was a *but*?"

Letty grinned as she reached for the falls of his trousers. "Because I know you," she said, fumbling with the buttons.

"Oh, my *God*," Vander groaned as her hand brushed the rock-hard bulge beneath the fabric. "I'm going to hell."

She had two buttons undone. "What makes you say that?"

"You're an... an innocent," he gasped.

"Not quite so innocent as I was ten minutes ago," she said cheerfully, releasing a third button. "You'll have to show me what to do. You don't mind, do you?"

"*Mind*?" He laughed. "No, I don't mind. God, this feels so wicked..."

"Which you probably like," Letty said, pulling open his falls.

"*Yes*." He was breathing hard. "I want to come so fucking much. I've been thinking about this all week."

A surge of excitement went through her. Vander had been thinking about *her*! It was her fondest dream come true.

She pressed a kiss against his neck. "Show me. I want to do this for you."

He slid her onto the seat of the swing so they were sitting side by side. It was snug, but they just fit.

He pushed his trousers low on his hips. Letty couldn't help but stare. Rising from a nest of black curls was his rod. She'd seen enough animals on the farm to know that this was the part that was meant to go inside of her, although it seemed awfully thick...

"Use your hand. Wrap it around me, and... *God*, your hands are soft!" he gasped.

A bead of moisture had formed at the tip of his member. Vander covered her hand with his own and guided her upward, moaning as she stroked that part of him. The liquid was exceptionally slick and made it easy to slide her hand up and down his length.

"Grip me tighter," he instructed, showing her the motion he liked. "That's it. God, Letty, you're going to make me come..."

She loved the way his eyes had gone unfocused with pleasure, the way his head lolled to the side. Encouraged, she kept up the motion he had shown her, sliding her hand all the way to the base of his shaft, then bringing it back up to caress the head, eliciting a moan she felt all the way in her stomach.

"Faster," Vander gasped. "Faster. Oh, *fuck*, Letty—you're going to make me come! That feels so good, that feels so *fucking* good, I'm... I'm... Oh, my *God*!"

He spread his legs wide just as he spasmed in her hand, sending a spurt of milky liquid spraying onto the ground. Letty continued stroking him as the white liquid emerged in pulses. She couldn't tear her eyes away from the fascinating sight.

Abruptly, Vander's hand covered hers. "That's good. That's perfect," he said. Letty looked up, and Vander had the most wonderful expression on his handsome face, happy and sleepy and almost dazed with pleasure.

Smiling, he kissed her deeply. "Thank you, Letty. That felt so fucking good."

"Good." Feeling delighted but also suddenly shy, she leaned her head against his shoulder. Vander wrapped an arm around her and kissed her temple, and they sat together in companionable silence.

After a few minutes, Vander groaned. "I'd better get you back to your family before you're missed."

Letty sighed. "You're probably right."

He pulled out his handkerchief, wiping her hand clean before seeing to himself. It took only a moment for them to restore themselves to rights, and the next thing she knew, Letty was walking down one of Vauxhall's graveled paths on Vander's arm, looking for all the world as if nothing had changed.

But really, everything had changed. At least, it had for her.

Glancing up at Vander's handsome profile, she wondered if anything had changed for him.

Chapter Nineteen

Two days later, Vander was ensconced in his closet at Beauclerk Marine Casualty, struggling to stay awake. He'd finally made it back to Boodle's to continue testing his plan to support himself by gambling. It had been a night of patient, methodical play, at the conclusion of which he'd been fourteen pounds richer than when he'd started.

This wasn't a bad thing. If he won big every night, no one would want to play with him. If he could average winnings of twenty-five pounds per night, that would yield an income of nine thousand a year.

Or, to be precise, 9125 pounds. Although who was counting?

To be sure, it had been a late night, and he was suffering from lack of sleep. But that wasn't the only reason for Vander's malaise this morning.

David had been right—Boodle's was dull. The extent to which he had enjoyed his best friend's company had masked how tedious the rest of it was. He'd thought he would find the mathematical analysis aspect of playing cards diverting, but the calculations were too simple to hold his interest.

Even worse, there had been another unpleasant incident last

night. It hadn't occurred at Vander's table, but at the next table over, some young idiot newly come into his fortune had bet—and lost—the funds intended for his sister's dowry. The whole club had heard him drunkenly sobbing about how his mother and sister would never forgive him as a footman showed him out.

It wasn't just young idiots. The talk that night had been about how Richard Clyde-Owens, who had once been a regular, had been forced to give up his membership. He'd reportedly had his personal effects seized by his creditors and been evicted from his London townhouse. The gossip was that he and his wife were now confined to a single room in a much less respectable part of town.

The thought occurred to Vander that even if he *could* make a living at the gaming tables, he wasn't sure that he *wanted* to. He could scarcely believe he was about to admit this, even to himself, but he found performing insurance analysis in this dreadful closet more enjoyable than spending his evenings at one of the most raucous gentlemen's clubs in London.

And more than that... Even if no one would look at him askance for winning the fortune of a Francis Llewellyn, or a Richard Clyde-Owens, or any man of their ilk who lacked the wit to know when to fold, Vander found he didn't have much stomach for it. He hadn't claimed Llewellyn's commission money yet, and now, he doubted he ever would. The disagreeable voice inside his head kept asking questions such as, *How does taking Francis Llewellyn's commission money make the world a better place?* And *Fifty years from now, do you think you'll be proud that this is what you did with your life?*

But the thing was, the work he was doing here, in his father's office? It *did* make the world a better place. Companies were willing to take risks when they knew that a lost ship wouldn't ruin them. Those risks allowed commerce to flow, to expand. And a rising economic tide lifted all boats.

Dear God—had he just quoted his father's speech on the

virtues of insurance? He half expected to hear the hoofbeats of four approaching horsemen, because if that wasn't a sign that the end times were upon them, he didn't know what was.

The door opened, and his father minced into the room. Cedric Beauclerk always looked excited to be at his insurance offices, but today, he looked like he was about to explode with enthusiasm.

"Good morning, Father." Vander took his spectacles off, then winced as he noticed the thick stack of folios his father carried. "Oh, dear—more files. I'll be hard-pressed to get through what you've already brought me."

"You've already been over most of these." His father settled one hip on the edge of the table. "These are the policies you pointed out to me last week. The Peruvian guano farmers sailing through Cape Horn that I had declined to quote. Per our discussion, I took another look at the numbers."

Vander leaned back, steepling his fingers. "And?"

His father adjusted his spectacles. "And I concluded that you were right. We have sufficient reserves to take on this risk. And there is an opportunity here. I ran the numbers again, and the rate I settled on was just about the one you had suggested—"

"Three times the rate around the Cape of Good Hope?"

"Just a hair over three times, yes. I sent the quotes out yesterday, unsure if anyone would be willing to pay such rates." He tapped the stack of files. "All six shipowners have already responded, accepting my quote. And word is getting around— I've already received inquiries about another three ships sailing for Callao." His father paused, his foot tapping excitedly in the air. "This is a significant opportunity to expand our business. One that I almost missed. But you saw it. I'm proud of you, son."

Vander smiled. Those were words he'd never thought to hear from his father. They felt... good. "Thank you, Father."

His father removed a few files from the top of the stack.

"These are the three ships that requested a quote. I thought I would let you take a stab at the analysis."

Vander put his spectacles back on. "I'd be glad to."

"Good." His father stood. "Work on them today, and we'll go over them together tomorrow."

"Very well."

His father was whistling as he left the room. Vander opened the top file, curious.

An hour later, he flipped the last file shut. He still had work to do, but he was optimistic that he was heading in the right direction. And the truth was...

This wasn't bad. He could see himself doing this for the rest of his life, much more easily than he could see himself wasting away at the tables at Boodle's. He would have to persuade his father to make a few changes. Open up a new office, one where sunlight occasionally fell upon the desk. Hire a private secretary so he could delegate the mundane tasks his father spent countless hours performing.

But, although the very notion had seemed unthinkable to him a few short weeks ago, Vander could almost see himself running Beauclerk Marine Casualty and acquiescing to his father's other demands.

All but for one thing.

Letty.

Prominent amongst his father's demands was that he settle down and marry. And much to his surprise, he could almost picture it. He could actually imagine himself giving up his degenerate lifestyle and spending the rest of his life with one woman.

But only if it was Letty. Letty was the central puzzle piece, and without her, nothing else fit.

And that was the rub, all right.

Because Letty was the one woman he could never have.

And if he couldn't have Letty, any chance of him being happy in the respectable life his father had planned for him crumbled to ashes.

But now that he thought on it, it was worse than that. Because the truth was, he hadn't been happy for some time. David had seen it before he had. Their whole rake-about-town routine had grown stale. The main thing he'd enjoyed about those wild nights was that he'd spent them with David.

The time had come for him to find something new. His father's ultimatum had merely led him to realize it a few months sooner than he otherwise would have.

But there was still a little nagging voice in the back of his head. One that said, *you thought you wanted all of those other women, too.* Mary Louise Huntley, Marguerite Cadieux, and the six other lovers the Brazen Belle had dredged up.

He had been so certain that each of them was the answer to his listlessness. But after he had slept with them, his interest had faded like drops of ink in a well.

What if it was the same with Letty? What if he married her then tired of her as surely as he'd tired of the rest of them?

That was the most terrifying possibility of all. It was one thing for his bad decision to ruin his own life. But the notion of ruining Letty's, of trapping her in an unhappy marriage, was far worse. Throw in the fact that he would irrevocably damage his friendship with David, and the notion of giving things a try with Letty became unthinkable.

The truth was, he wasn't going to be happy whether he accepted his father's deal or not.

He'd made a hash of everything.

And he had no one to blame but himself.

Chapter Twenty

That evening, Emily's parents collected Letty and took her to Mrs. Ridley's rout. Once they arrived, Emily and Letty found a private alcove where they could talk.

In hushed whispers, Letty told her friend everything—and she did mean *everything*—that had passed between her and Vander at Vauxhall.

"But this is wonderful news!" Emily hissed. "He must have feelings for you, too."

Letty's shoulders slumped. "I doubt it. He has this notion that, by showing me what a *proper* kiss should be like, I might be able to coax whichever man I eventually marry into doing a better job of it. When he kissed me in the garden, he came out and told me that was the only reason he was doing it."

Emily frowned. "Did he say so last night?"

"No. But I'm sure he was just carrying the exercise to its logical conclusion."

"Hmm." Judging by her pursed lips and sideways look, Emily was not convinced. "Then he did not seem... *stirred*... by the encounter?"

Letty's cheeks were aflame. "I'm sure I don't know what you mean."

"Did he have an erec—"

"*Emily!*" Letty stuck her head out of the alcove and hastily scanned the area to make sure no one had moved into hearing distance. Once she was satisfied, she ducked back in, glowering at her friend. "How can you ask such a question?"

Emily's expression was triumphant. "I see that the answer is yes."

"You don't know that!"

"Oh, but I do. Because I know you, Letty. And right now, you are embarrassed. Had he not had a commensurate response to your own, that would be evidence that he felt nothing for you, in which case you would not be embarrassed. You would be *despondent.*"

Letty rubbed her temple. "Sometimes I wish you were not quite so insightful. *Fine.* If you must know, he did seem... interested."

"I knew it! And that is why you must *act.*"

"Act?" Letty blinked at her friend. "What would you have me do?"

"Seduce him." Emily said this in the same voice one would say *pass the salt,* as if it were a straightforward, obvious endeavor.

"How on earth am I to do that?" Letty hissed.

Emily waved a hand. "You'll figure it out."

Letty's cheeks were burning. "I am fairly certain that I will not!"

Emily cast her eyes heavenward. "He's a *rake.* Just arrange an assignation, make it clear that you are willing, and he will take care of the rest."

"And what if you're wrong? What if he doesn't have feelings for me, too?" Letty's heart was racing just imagining the humiliation.

"The way I see it, there are three possible outcomes. One, that he returns your feelings, you make love, and he proposes."

"Which is never going to happen," Letty muttered.

Emily ignored her. "Two, that he does not return your feelings, but is willing to make love to you in the interest of educating you, so you can better instruct your future husband. If that should be the case, answer me this—would you rather have one night with Vander? Or would it be more painful in the end?"

Letty frowned, considering. "I... I would rather have one night with Vander."

Emily nodded. "That's what I thought. The third possibility is that he declines to make love to you. Which would be humiliating. But answer me this—which would be worse? The possibility of his rejection, or having to wonder for the rest of your life what might have been had you summoned the courage to ask?"

Letty rubbed her temple. "I don't know. Must you ask such difficult questions?"

"I must," Emily insisted. "Because, don't you see, Letty? Your brother and parents are traveling. You have the run of the house to yourself. All you have to do is steal him into your bedroom. You will not have an opportunity like this again, and that is why you must do this *tonight*."

"*Tonight*?" Now Letty's heart was threatening to pound right out of her chest. "But I can't... I don't... What if there's a baby?" she hissed. "Whichever of my suitors I accept in the end, I cannot go to the altar carrying another man's child!"

Emily nodded sagely. "You're right. You'll have to take precautions."

Letty squinted at her friend. "Precautions? What precautions? What are you talking about?"

Emily leaned in to whisper, "Do you remember when we were snooping in David's room? We were about fourteen, and we found those strange translucent tubes with a pink ribbon around one end?"

"Yes. But what does that have to do with—"

"I recently learned what those are. They're called sheaths. Men place them over their, um... *appendages*, in order to prevent conception. And also the transmission of diseases."

Letty stared at her friend in horror. "Emily, do you mean to tell me that you and David have—"

"No." Now it was Emily's turn to blush. "I would've told you if we had. We've done less than you and Vander, to be honest. But David told me about the sheaths because his past is not materially different from Vander's, and he wanted to reassure me that he had taken precautions. I put two and two together and realized that the thing he was describing was those little tubes we found."

Letty was so embarrassed she didn't know where to look. "What are you suggesting I do?"

"Sneak into David's room and take one."

Letty couldn't believe she was even having this absurd conversation. "This is all moot because Vander isn't here tonight. I have no way of arranging this assignation you've so carefully planned."

"So, send him a note. And do it tonight." Emily leaned in. "Aren't your parents returning tomorrow?"

"They are," Letty admitted.

"So? Are you going to do it?"

Letty squeezed her eyes shut. "I—I don't know. I'll have to think on it."

Emily held up both hands. "That's all I ask."

They lapsed into silence. Letty knew already that she wouldn't be able to carry the simplest conversation for the rest of the ball, with these thoughts churning around in her head. What on earth was she going to do?

She would regret throwing away a chance to be with Vander. Of that, she had no doubt.

But was it worth the humiliation if he should reject her?

And what if she should find herself with child? She might not love Bertie or Lord Throckmorton. But they did not deserve to be deceived in that regard.

Emily cleared her throat, recalling her to the alcove in which they stood. "Say, do you think David knows about that spot that you mentioned? And the thing Vander did? With his tongue?"

Letty whipped her head around to gaze at her friend in horror. "I can assure you, I have not discussed such things with my *brother*."

Emily waved a hand. "That's fair. I can understand that would be awkward." She paused, but only for the space of one breath. "But perhaps you could ask Vander to speak with him and explain—"

Letty put her fingers in her ears. "Absolutely not. I know you find him dashing, but I have no wish to think about my brother in that capacity. You will have to mention it to him yourself."

"Please, Letty?"

"No!"

"But if the act was as pleasurable as you say, I want to make sure that—"

"What can you two be discussing that has you so engrossed?"

Letty and Emily leaped apart as Emily's mother poked her head into the alcove. "Nothing!" they shrieked in high-pitched unison.

"Hmmm." Judging by Mrs. Arbuthnot's bland expression, it did not appear that they had been overheard. "Lord Throckmorton was looking for you, Letty. The dancing is about to begin."

And so, Letty abandoned the alcove. It was fortunate that her dance was with the baron and not with Bertie, as it meant there was no conversation she had to keep up with. As it was, she spent the evening in a state of anxious distraction.

Chapter Twenty-One

In the end, Letty decided to send the note.

She found a writing desk in the corner of an empty parlor and scrawled a quick message while Emily stood guard. She then slipped it to a boy who was loitering out front in hopes that someone might hire him to perform just such an errand, along with a penny.

Vander, I need your help. Meet me at my house, but don't come to the front door. Sneak into the gardens. I'll meet you there at midnight.
Letty

At five minutes before the appointed hour, she slipped down the back stairs unnoticed. Now there was nothing left to do but stand wringing her hands in the shadows to see if he would come.

There were a thousand reasons he might not. Vander might be out tonight. Or maybe he would receive her note but decide he had better things to do. The boy might have taken her penny and thrown the note into the gutter. The boy might have tried and failed to find the right address. She might have given him the wrong address, because, of course, she had never been to Vander's bachelor apartments. But David had once mentioned that he had a large first-floor suite at the Albany, and naturally, she had committed it to memory because she was pathetic when it came to anything relating to Vander, and—

A soft creak pierced the night sounds of the garden. Letty's eyes shot to the garden gate, which was swinging open. A familiar head of tousled black hair appeared around the edge of the door.

"Vander!" she hissed. "Over here."

As he moved to shut the door, Letty reminded herself how happy she was that he had come. It was perfectly normal to feel incandescently happy and as if you might cast your accounts, simultaneously and in equal measure.

Apparently.

She marked the flare of recognition in his eyes as he picked her out in the shadows. He hurried over. "Letty, what's wrong? Are you in danger?"

"Nothing like that," she reassured him. "I just..." She swallowed thickly, gathering her courage. "I need to ask a favor of you."

"Of course." He stared down at her in the moonlight, waiting for her to elaborate.

"Um... why don't we go up to my room?"

Vander's soft laugh echoed against the garden walls. "I may not be an expert on propriety, but even I know I can't set foot in your room."

"It's all right. My parents and brother are all away, remember? So there's no one on the second floor. So long as we manage to slip past the servants, no one will know you're there."

Vander's expression was pained. "Still, I'm not sure it's a good idea."

Letty's nostrils flared. Of all the times for him to become

concerned about propriety! She struggled to sound nonchalant as she asked, "Whyever not? If no one but us knows about it—"

"It would be too tempting," Vander said, a note of finality in his voice.

This was both good and bad. Good because he actually found her tempting! But bad in that he seemed determined to resist this temptation.

Letty forced herself to lift her chin rather than cringe. It was time to lay her cards on the table. "That isn't a problem. The temptation to which you refer is the very reason I summoned you tonight."

Vander's eyes flew open. "Letty, I... I think I misunderstood."

She grabbed his hand and started for the house, relieved that he stumbled after her without complaint. "You did not misunderstand. You understood perfectly." She paused just shy of the door. "Now hush. The servants are having a gathering downstairs. It was noisy when I slipped out, so I don't think they'll hear us, but we should be careful all the same."

"Careful," Vander muttered as she led him inside. "It doesn't strike me that there's anything careful about—"

"Quiet!" Letty hissed as they came to the back stairs. From below came the sounds of clapping, accompanied by a solitary fiddle. Seeing no one about, Letty hustled him up two flights of stairs.

She poked her head into the hallway and peered about. Seeing no one there, she dragged Vander to her room at the end of the hall and shoved him inside.

"I shouldn't be here," Vander murmured even as he glanced around her room, curious. "This is a terrible idea. What the..." He blanched as he noticed the sheath Letty had stolen from David's bedroom, which was sitting on her bedside table.

Vander ran a hand over his face. "You're serious about this."

"Of course, I am." Letty thought she might die of mortification, but she forced herself to ask, "Do you not want to?"

Vander's response was a startled laugh, which Letty did not find entirely flattering. "Do you have the faintest idea what it is you're proposing we do?"

"I do!" Letty protested, then added weakly, "Theoretically."

"Because if you knew the first thing about the act, then you wouldn't have to ask. Just one look at me and you would know that I'm *interested*."

In her embarrassment, Letty had been keeping her gaze fixed upon the wall behind his head. Now she chanced a glance at him, her eyes going immediately to the falls of his trousers.

"Oh, my gracious!" Surely enough, there was a large bulge tenting Vander's falls, suggesting that he was more than slightly *interested*.

Letty cleared her throat. Goodness, but this was awkward! "What's the problem, then?"

Vander cast his eyes to the heavens. "I wouldn't describe it as a *problem*, per se. Not for me, in any case. But there are a variety of disastrous outcomes that might befall you."

"That's why I have the, um..." Letty gestured to the translucent tube she had pilfered from David's room. "What is it properly called?"

Vander groaned, then placed his hands on her shoulders. "Letty, this is precisely why I can't make love to you. You scarcely know what it is you're asking for."

"And that is precisely why you should make love to me!" Letty shot back. "If my first lover is not you, then it will be either Bertie Strickleton or Lord Throckmorton. Does either strike you as the type to unlock the secrets of a woman's pleasure?"

Vander shifted awkwardly. "Um..."

"No. You know full well they are not. Bertie never thinks of anyone but himself. And, in the unlikely event that he felt inclined to do anything for me, he probably wouldn't have the faintest idea how to go about it. Meanwhile, I doubt it has occurred to Lord Throckmorton that a woman might find pleasure in the act, or that he should make it his concern."

Judging by Vander's guilty expression, her assessment was spot on.

She looped her arms up around his neck. "And that is why I need you, Vander. Because you're right—I am ignorant. And, if you will not help me, I am doomed to remain ignorant, and I might go my entire life without experiencing this."

She closed the distance between them, pressing her body against his. He groaned, his head lolling back. She felt him shift his hips, unable to stop himself from rubbing against her softness.

She almost had him. "Please, Vander? Please, won't you show me?"

He pulled away, and Letty's heart sank. But then she noticed that he had gone to scoop up the sheath. Walking over to her washstand, he poured a little water from the ewer into the basin and dropped the sheath in.

"Vander?" she asked uncertainly.

He looked up from prodding the sheath with his finger. "You have to soak them in water before you use them."

"Does that mean we're going to use it?" she blurted. She felt her cheeks flame.

Vander smiled as he crossed back over to her. Taking her in his arms, he kissed her ear. "As if I could deny you."

And then his lips found hers. This kiss was different from the ones they'd previously shared. She had thought those kisses had been scorching in their intensity, but they didn't hold a candle to this one. Vander devoured her, completely and utterly, and Letty had no thought of asking him to stop. Her heart was racing, her body was trembling, and when her knees gave out, he scooped her up and carried her to the bed.

She was dressed for bed in her night rail and wrapper with her hair in a plait. Vander groaned as he opened her outer robe like he was unwrapping a present, leaving her in only a thin linen nightgown. He tugged the ribbon from the bottom of her plait and began undoing it. Once her hair was falling down her back in waves, he rose from the bed.

His eyes never leaving her, he unknotted his cravat with hands that weren't entirely steady. He stripped to his shirtsleeves, then sat on the edge of the bed.

Vander glanced around her room as he pulled off his boots. "I really wish we had some oil, especially as this is your first time. I don't suppose you have anything like that?"

Letty wracked her brain. "Just the coconut oil I use on my hair."

Vander glanced at her and grinned. "You have coconut oil? That's perfect." He padded over to her dressing table. "Where is it?"

"It's in the little tin on the left side... Yes, that one."

He deposited the tin on her bedside table, then crawled up the bed to join her. He wore nothing but an open-necked shirt and trousers, and Letty trembled as he took her into his arms. "I want to make this beautiful for you," he whispered.

He kissed her again, but it wasn't enough for either of them, and his hands soon strayed to her breasts. He somehow unerringly found the places that made her squirm upon the bed. By the time he moved his mouth down to kiss her through the fine linen of her nightgown, she was crying out for him.

He pulled the ribbon tie at the neck of her night rail, then pushed it down around her shoulders. Her bust was distinctly modest in size, but Vander made an appreciative sound as her breasts came into view. "So beautiful," he murmured, kissing her throat and moving his hands to cup her.

He had touched her there the other night at Vauxhall, but this was more intense. He had better access, for one. But also, something about the sight of Vander's strong hands touching her roused Letty even higher. How many hours had she spent dreaming of this moment that was finally coming true?

He kissed his way across her collarbone and replaced his hands with his lips. He started by pressing soft kisses all over her chest, which made her breath come fast, and when he finally sucked a nipple between his lips, Letty's back arched upon the bed and her fingers raked through his thick black hair.

He repeated the same delicious torture on the other side, until she was squirming upon the bed. She heard his voice as if from far away. "Lift your hips. That's it." She realized he was stripping her of her nightgown, which would leave her fully exposed to his gaze, but she was too lost in a haze of pleasure to feel embarrassed about it.

He started to join her on the mattress, but Letty stopped him with a hand to his chest. "Wait."

She wasn't the only one whose breath was coming fast. "What is it?"

Flushing, she tugged at the hem of his shirt. "Take this off. I want to see... you know."

That earned her a smile. He pushed himself up to kneeling and peeled the shirt up over his head. Letty felt her mouth go a little bit dry. She had secretly wondered if the Brazen Belle's assertion that women fell into a swoon at the sight of Vander's shirtless form in the boxing ring had been an exaggeration.

She could easily believe it, now that she was seeing him in the flesh. He wasn't overly bulky, but there wasn't an ounce of fat on him. Corded muscles stretched the length of his arms, then swelled through the breadth of his shoulders. His stomach was no less gorgeous, with little rows of square muscles that disappeared beneath the waistband of his trousers, just as a trail of black hair cropped up on his stomach.

He was exquisite enough to put the discus thrower at the British Museum to shame.

She reached a tentative hand toward his chest, then paused.

Vander chuckled. "Touch me everywhere," he said, pressing her hand against his stomach.

Letty couldn't help but give a start. His stomach was hard as marble, yet warm. She stroked up his chest, marveling that his body could be so different from hers.

Vander groaned, rolling onto the bed and scooping her up in his arms.

Letty gave a startled gasp of pleasure as all of his smooth, warm skin came into contact with hers. "V-Vander!" she gasped.

"I have good news for you."

"What's that?" she breathed.

He kissed her soundly on the lips, and his voice was as dark as midnight as he said, "It's time for the good part."

He took control then, giving her a kiss worthy of the most wicked rake in London. His hands roved the length of her body, finding tender spots she hadn't known existed.

By the time he started kissing his way down her body, her skin was flushed and her heart was flying. That place between her legs was throbbing like a heartbeat, and she held her breath as he trailed a hand ever so slowly across her stomach.

He sat up just long enough to snag the little tin of coconut oil from her bedside table. Slicking some over his fingers, he delved between her legs.

He had incinerated every fiber of her maidenly modesty, as was evidenced by the fact that her thighs fell open for him without the slightest hesitation. But strangely, she didn't feel embarrassed. Being here with Vander felt like the most natural thing in the world.

It felt... *right*.

His thumb settled upon that little pearl between her legs, the one he had titillated to such good effect on the swing at Vauxhall. And—*dear* God—she could see why he had wanted to use the coconut oil. It made his fingers slick and delicious, even better than they had been when he had touched her for the first time.

This time, he slid a finger inside of her as well. Which felt... curious. Thanks to the coconut oil, it slid in easily, and there wasn't any pain, at least, not yet. Just a sensation of being stretched.

She could not help but wonder, if his solitary finger felt so tight, how was it possible that his member was going to fit? She had held it in her hand at Vauxhall, after all, and knew it to be significantly bigger than a finger.

Vander pressed a kiss against her temple. "Stop thinking."

Letty gave a startled laugh. "Easier said than done."

She felt him smile against her skin. "I can help you with that."

Then he slid down the bed, positioning his head between the apex of her thighs and pressing them open. Gently, far too gently, he started flicking his tongue over that magic little spot. It felt so good, Letty shot up on the bed, sitting halfway up before collapsing back on the mattress.

He brought his hands to the petals that surrounded her opening and proceeded to touch every inch of them with a stroke that was half caress, half massage.

It felt *so good*, divine, really, and yet Letty's fingers were fisting in his thick, dark hair. Because she needed him to go faster, to give her more, at that little spot he was circling with his tongue.

"Vander!" she gasped. "Vander, *please!*"

He responded by removing his tongue from that spot, but only to trace great circles around it. Letty desperately tried to pull him back to the place she was discovering she needed him the most, but he continued to torment her.

After a few minutes of torture, he finally brought his tongue back to that magical nub, and Letty cried out, the pleasure was so intense. Now he was going slightly faster, laving her with the flat of his tongue, and she could feel herself climbing toward that peak she had reached for the first time at Vauxhall. She barely had the presence of mind to note Vander sliding a finger, then two, into her passage. This time, they slid in smoothly, with no resistance, although she did feel pleasantly full.

"Oh, Vander!" she cried. "I'm so close! I'm so—"

Suddenly, he stopped using his tongue altogether, and Letty cried out in frustration. But her torment only lasted a moment, because Vander was only changing position. He brought his lips around that wonderful little spot.

And then, he started to *suck*.

Letty understood in an instant why those eight women Vander had seduced and abandoned had been disconsolate.

Because this was the purest, most unadulterated form of pleasure on the face of this earth. There was nothing, nothing in the world, that could compare to the absolute bliss Vander was giving her between her thighs. She felt drunk on it, knew nothing but the pleasure as he carried her higher, and higher, and—and—

Letty screamed when she came. She clapped a hand over her mouth afterward, because—the servants! But she couldn't help it. She had no control over her body. Her thighs were shaking almost violently, her hips were bucking off the bed, and every inch of her was trembling, other than the area between her thighs, which was squeezing in pulse after rhythmic pulse.

The next thing Letty was conscious of was Vander sliding up and taking her in his arms. He had removed his trousers, and Letty groaned at the feeling of all of his warm skin pressed against hers. She could feel the hard ridge of his cock pressing against her stomach, but he just held her, making no move to do something to relieve his own ache.

After the room stopped spinning, Letty said, "I thought we were going to make love."

She felt Vander smile against her cheek. "We are making love. What we just did is part of lovemaking, and don't let anyone tell you otherwise. It just happens that we're not finished yet."

"Good," Letty said fiercely, burying her face in his neck. God, she loved the familiar scent of his cinnamon-and-ginger shaving tonic and the slight rasp of his shaved cheek against hers...

He kissed her cheek. "I'll go and get ready for the rest of it."

He rose from the bed and padded over to the washstand. She

watched in fascination as he fished the sheath out of the basin, dried it on a towel, and slid it over his engorged shaft. He made quick work of the ribbons at the base of the sheath, then returned to the bed.

He took another dollop of coconut oil from the tin and smoothed it up and down his own length. His eyes went slightly glassy as he stroked himself, and Letty propped herself up on one elbow, enjoying the look of pleasure written so clearly on his face.

He climbed back onto the bed and pulled her into his arms. Letty tried to enjoy his embrace, but now that the moment had come, the moment in which he would claim her maidenhead, she couldn't help but feel nervous.

"Stop thinking," Vander whispered in her ear again.

"I can't," Letty protested, then pulled back enough to peer at him. "Wait... how did you know?"

Vander ran a warm hand down the length of her spine. "You're stiff as a board. Let's see if I can't fix that."

Sitting up, he flipped her onto her stomach. He proceeded to caress every inch of her backside, starting with her scalp and finishing with her toes. He then repeated the process, this time scouring her scalp with his fingernails, then kneading and massaging the rest of the way down.

Letty groaned, it felt so wonderful. And it did indeed have the effect of helping her relax.

But as he reached her bottom and began to squeeze and stroke her there, she noticed an additional effect.

She had started to feel aroused again.

As Vander moved down her thighs, she began to squirm on the bed, searching for a little friction. Her efforts were in vain.

By the time he reached her calves, she was breathing hard.

By the time he began to massage her feet, she was making the most embarrassing sounds.

Completing his ministrations, Vander moved back up to sit beside her. But he didn't flip her over, as she had expected.

Instead, he reached between her legs, exploring her folds as he had done before. Letty cried out as he gave her the touch she had been craving for some time.

"Aha!" She could hear the smug satisfaction in Vander's voice. "Just as I suspected."

"*Please*, Vander!" were the only words she could manage.

He did flip her over then and settled between her thighs. His weight on top of her felt delicious. Reaching for the little tin of coconut oil, he slicked his cock once again, then positioned himself at her entrance. Letty was so far gone with desire, and so boneless from the massage he had given her minutes ago, she didn't even tense up.

Then Vander was sliding forward. It felt strange, having his thickness inside of her. She felt... full. Stretched, even. But...

"Vander!" she gasped, realizing that he was fully sheathed. "It... it didn't hurt!"

He brushed her fringe back from her forehead. "No?" His voice sounded strained.

She gave an experimental wiggle. "Not really. I feel... very full. But I wouldn't say that it hurts."

He kissed her temple. "That's wonderful. I'm going to try moving now. Let me know if it's too much."

Letty nodded, biting her lip. She felt herself start to tense again.

But before Vander moved, he threaded an arm between their bodies and brought his thumb to that magical spot between her legs. He started tracing small circles there, and Letty moaned, it felt so good.

Only then did he withdraw most of the way, then slowly press forward. All the time he kept his thumb busy titillating her.

"Oh, *Vander*!" she groaned.

He laughed, a breathless sound. "Oh, Letty," he replied, slowly withdrawing and sliding back in. "Is it all right if I move a little more?"

It was the strangest thing, but his cock inside of her didn't feel overly tight anymore. Her passage was entirely slick, between the wetness between her legs and the coconut oil. In truth... she didn't feel all that much, either in terms of pain or pleasure, from Vander's cock moving inside her.

His thumb on her little rosebud, on the other hand...

"Go ahead," she gasped as his fingers traced a wicked figure eight that made her hips buck.

And so he proceeded. She loved having Vander's weight upon her, loved the way his body rubbed against hers, loved hearing him groan in her ear as his pleasure built and built.

And she especially loved the way he was stroking her between her thighs.

The pleasure became almost unbearable. Letty felt like she was going to shatter. Her body started to quiver, and her thighs started to shake. "Vander!" she gasped. "Vander, I'm... I'm..."

He swirled his thumb faster, and the bliss swept over Letty like a wave, pulling her under. She was vaguely conscious of her thighs spasming uncontrollably as she clung desperately to his shoulders.

He was thrusting fast and hard, and she felt him go rigid in her arms. "Letty. Oh, my... Oh, *fuck... Letty*!"

Then it was his turn to shudder in her arms while grunting a mixture of curses and endearments.

Eventually, he slumped down on top of her, breathing hard, his head resting beside hers on the pillow. His eyes were closed, but he looked drowsy and happy and deliciously rumpled. Letty traced patterns over the satiny skin of his back, which was damp with the barest sheen of sweat.

The moment was indescribably sweet. She had literally been dreaming of it for half her life.

And yet, she couldn't seem to silence the nagging little voice that wondered whether this would be the only such moment she and Vander would ever have.

Chapter Twenty-Two

I t took Vander a few minutes to summon the wherewithal to lift his head. Letty smiled up at him, but it was a tremulous sort of smile as if she were in danger of bursting into tears.

"How are you?" he asked gently, smoothing a lock of hair back from her face.

"Wonderful," she answered. He could see that she meant it. He supposed it was natural for one's emotions to be overflowing after your first time making love.

Come to think of it, he was in uncharted waters, too. He hadn't known it could be like that, hadn't known it was possible to feel such a connection with his partner.

Letty gave a shuddering breath beneath him. "I must be crushing you," he said, propping himself up on one elbow.

"It's fine. No, it's not fine—what a tepid word for the most marvelous feeling." She wrapped her arms around his back and pulled him down again. "I wish we could stay here forever."

Vander smiled against her temple. "Me, too."

He froze. Because... he meant that.

He, who had grown tired of his previous eight paramours the

moment they'd finished copulating, didn't want to leave. He genuinely wanted to stay here with Letty.

Forever.

He didn't even care if they didn't make love. Which wasn't to say that he didn't want to make love to her again. He very much did.

His cock was already at half-mast inside of her, clearly interested in the prospect.

But, given that this was her first time, it was probably best not to push things. And... he didn't mind. He really didn't. He just wanted to hold her in his arms, to talk with her, laugh with her. He wanted her to fall asleep on his shoulder and wake beside him in the morning. He wanted to have breakfast with her at that little table by the window, her in her wrapper and him in his banyan.

And then, he wanted to repeat this process every day for the rest of his life.

He sat up enough to look at her again. He felt dizzy with these unfamiliar thoughts swirling around inside his head.

He reminded himself that this was *not* why Letty had asked him to come tonight. She had specifically asked him to teach her how to find her pleasure. He knew what he should do, and that was to tell her to make sure her future husband attended to that little spot between her legs he had rubbed with his thumb. That if her husband expected to do nothing more than the things that felt good for him, it was highly unlikely that Letty would find equal enjoyment... at least, in Vander's experience, which was considerable.

But he found that he couldn't bear to utter a word of that. Because the thought of Letty having a husband other than him was *agonizing*.

He found her smiling up at him, brown eyes sparkling. She reached up and smoothed her fingers through his hair. "You somehow manage to look even more handsome when your hair's a mess. Meanwhile, I probably look like Medusa. It's positively unfair."

His heart thumped so hard he was surprised it wasn't audible. And he realized—

He *loved* her. He didn't just desire Letty, want to make love to her.

He'd gone and fallen in love with her.

Hellfire and damnation. This whole situation was a thousand times worse than he'd realized. He'd just about resigned himself to a dreary existence, toiling away in his assigned closet at his father's office, married to a woman he tolerated but didn't care for.

That sounded barely endurable. But when you tossed in the fact that he would *be without the woman he loved*, the whole situation became untenable.

Unless... what if *Letty* could be the woman he married?

Her parents would refuse their permission. And David would never speak to him again.

But he thought Letty might—*might*—say yes. After all, she had agreed to accept one of her two suitors, and she wasn't particularly enthusiastic about either of her options.

He wasn't a great prospect, either, given his past. But she liked him. He knew she did. And he was bloody rich and good at giving her orgasms.

And she liked his hair.

That had to count for something...

"Vander?" Letty's voice pierced his scattered thoughts. "Is everything all right?"

He struggled to attend. What had she been saying? Oh, yes, she had compared herself to... Medusa, and he hadn't spoken a word of denial.

He brushed a kiss across her forehead. "You look nothing like Medusa. You'd make Aphrodite sick with envy."

It occurred to him that he was still inside her and the sheath was full, and he should clean himself up before disaster struck. Withdrawing, he padded over to the washstand.

His thoughts were flying away with him. A vision of his future was slowly coming into focus. With a few changes, work at his father's insurance company would be tolerable.

But he had to have Letty as his wife. That part was non-negotiable.

He returned to the bed and took her in his arms, pulling the counterpane up over them. Now he just needed to convince her parents that he was worthy of their one and only daughter...

Something occurred to him. "When is the ball when you have to announce which one of your suitors you're going to marry?"

Letty yawned against his shoulder. "It's tomorrow. Or—I suppose by now it's today."

Vander sat halfway up. "Today? You mean it's in sixteen hours?" He threw off the covers and stood, scooping his scattered garments from off the floor.

"Vander?" Letty propped herself up on one elbow. Her hair was sticking out to the side and his heart squeezed, she looked so adorable. "What's wrong?"

That would be the fact that he had less than twenty-four hours to convince her parents that he was good enough for their only daughter. What he needed was a plan, and a damn good one, and he sure as hell wasn't going to be able to think straight with Letty lying naked in his arms.

But he could hardly tell her that, so he settled for, "Nothing," as he pulled on his trousers. Seeing Letty's frown, he added, "I just... can't be discovered here. You would be—"

"Ruined," she said along with him. "I understand," she added, although she didn't look happy about it.

Vander paused, his fingers upon the buttons of his waistcoat. Should he say something to Letty? Offer her some reassurance?

He decided against it. He needed to do a damn sight better than a slapdash proposal in her bedroom while he was halfway out the door. He'd made a complete hash of things so far. Looking back, he cringed as he remembered the night he'd asked Letty for her help, and she'd clearly thought he was proposing.

Letty deserved to feel *treasured*.

He pulled on his boots. He needed a ring. And... some flowers. Yes, flowers were good. And... bloody hell, he wasn't sure what else, but there was going to have to be more to it than a ring and some flowers...

He had just tugged his coat into place and was starting for the door when a small voice behind him interrupted his train of thought.

"Vander?"

He turned to find Letty peering up at him from beneath the snow-white counterpane, which she'd drawn up to her chin. She looked... sad.

"Is that it, then?" she asked, her voice cracking.

He crossed the room in three strides, sat on the bed, and pulled her into his arms. He proceeded to kiss her as if the room was on fire around them and it was going to be the last thing he ever did. He poured every ounce of love he felt for her into it, but make no mistake, it was not a sweet sort of kiss. It was a wicked kiss, the kiss of a rakehell, that bespoke every deliciously depraved act he was going to perform upon her body the second they were man and wife.

When he finally lifted his head, they were both breathing hard. "Does that answer your question?"

Letty really was adorable when she was confused. "Yes. No. I —I'm not sure."

He stroked his fingertips along the edge of her beautiful face. "No, Letty, that is not it. I will call upon you tomorrow. And we'll talk."

"Can't we talk now?" she blurted.

He pressed a kiss into the palm of her hand, then stood. "No. I have a few things I must do first."

"At two o'clock in the morning?" she asked, glancing around as if his intended task would present itself there in her bedroom.

"Actually, yes." He was going to be up half the night planning, after all. "Until tomorrow. Good night, my darling."

"D-darling?" she sputtered. "Did you just call me—"

But Vander was already halfway out the door. He had planning to do.

Chapter Twenty-Three

Vander started with his own father.

He was fully prepared for his father to argue with him. But once Vander finished laying out his conditions for joining Beauclerk Marine Casualty, his father fell silent, steepling his fingers and staring sightlessly at the wall behind Vander's shoulder.

After a few minutes, Vander could take the suspense no longer. "Well, Father?"

"I think," his father said slowly, "it's a brilliant idea."

Vander almost fell off his chair. "You... you do?"

His father nodded crisply, suddenly certain. "I do. The truth is, Evander, the business has stagnated these last few years. I have a certain way I like to do things, but I believe that I have carried the company as far as it can go doing things my way. I'll be honest— your proposals seem odd to me. But I think it might be akin to your suggestion that we form a high-risk pool for the Cape Horn route. I think perhaps it is time I tried something different, and you are just the person to help me with that."

Vander smiled. "Thank you, Father."

～

His next stop was at his parents' London mansion. "Maman," he said as he strode into the morning room, "will you come with me to Rundell and Bridge?"

His mother looked up from the letter she had been penning, her eyes keen at the mention of London's most prominent jeweler. "Just what do you wish to purchase at Rundell and Bridge?"

He braced himself. "A ring. I've decided to propose to Let—"

Somehow, she was up from her chair and across the room, framing his face before he could finish saying her name. "I knew my son was not the stupidest man in all of London! This is the best news, Vander, the very best!"

He smiled softly. "I'm glad you approve. I was hoping you could help me pick something. You know a thousand times more about jewelry than I do."

"Yes, it is fortunate that you came to me first." His mother wrinkled her nose. "They will have nothing at Rundell and Bridge. Nothing at all."

Vander's lips twitched. Being from India, his mother tended to find the selection of gemstones available in Europe uninspiring, to say the least. "The jeweler to His Majesty the King doesn't have a single ring?"

She was already striding toward the door. "Not one *we* would ever consider, and what they will have ready-made will be even worse. But don't worry." She cast him a brilliant smile. "I have just the thing."

～

His mother was right—they didn't have anything ready-made at Rundell and Bridge that was up to Vander's standards. But his mother donated some gems from her personal collection, and the jewelers were able to set them on short notice. In the end, Vander was quite happy with the resulting ring. He was confident Letty was going to love it, and he couldn't wait to give it to her.

But before he could, the most significant obstacle of all remained.

He arrived at Daughtry House at noon. The family butler, Henderson, personally took his hat. "I'm afraid Lord Trundley has not yet returned from his travels."

"I'm actually here to see Lord and Lady Baldridge, if they will receive me." Vander dropped his voice to a whisper. "It is imperative that Lady Leticia not know that I am here."

"Conveniently, she is out with Miss Arbuthnot," Henderson said. "Let me see if the earl and countess are available."

They were, and they received him in the morning room. "Vander," Lord Baldridge said, coming over to shake his hand. He gestured for Vander to take a seat on the yellow silk sofa. He and Lady Baldridge settled into the chairs opposite him. "To what do we owe the pleasure?"

Vander shifted his weight around, although, in truth, no change of position would render him comfortable. He'd stayed up most of the night, trying to figure out what he could say to convince the earl and countess to allow him to marry Letty.

He'd only been able to come up with one approach that had even a prayer of success. It was unpalatable.

But it was his only shot.

Steeling himself, he said, "I'll just come out and say it. The reason I have called upon you today is to inform you that I have ruined your daughter."

Lady Baldridge made a sound that was half gasp and half shriek, one hand flying to her heart.

Beside her, Lord Baldridge surged to his feet. "What is the meaning of this?"

Vander held out his hands. "I'm sorry to have shocked you.

But it's important that you know the unvarnished truth. Letty is ruined. Completely and irrevocably."

Lady Baldridge looked horrified. "Why are you telling us this?"

"Because I know that, under normal circumstances, you would never allow Letty to marry someone like me. What I am trying to communicate is that these are not normal circumstances. You *must* give your blessing to the match. There is no other way."

The fist Lord Baldridge had been shaking at him suddenly sagged. "You mean... you want to marry her?"

"I do," Vander said firmly. "I want to spend the rest of my life with her. I know you will have trouble believing it, but I will be a good husband to her."

The earl's anger and the countess's panic had evaporated. "Well, then," Lord Baldridge said, resuming his seat. "That's all right. Not quite the order I would've wanted you to take things in. But it all comes out right in the end, I suppose."

Lady Baldridge looked positively giddy. "I can't believe it. Letty will be delighted!"

Vander studied them, looking for any sign of second thoughts. "I am pleased to see that you have resigned yourself to the match. You must not think of changing your mind. You see, I have not merely compromised your daughter. When I say that she is ruined, I mean—"

The earl held a hand out and gave an awkward chuckle. "That —that's all right, son. We don't need to hear the details."

"Oh, dear!" Lady Baldridge exclaimed. "Letty is expected to announce her decision tonight at the Sunderland ball. You'll need to ask her before then."

"I will," Vander agreed. "In fact, I have something particular in mind. And I'm going to need your help."

Chapter Twenty-Four

etty was having a strange afternoon.

When she got home from Emily's house, her mother was waiting for her. "Come, Letty. You need to dress for Lady Sunderland's ball."

"Do I?" Letty checked the clock in the entryway. "It's only half four. Surely I have another hour before I need to—"

Her mother seized her wrist and began towing her up the stairs. "Right now. Every eye will be upon you tonight. You must look your very best."

Letty sighed but didn't argue.

When they got to her room, Letty saw that her maid, Sarah, had already laid out a gown. It was the same dress she'd been wearing the night Vander first approached her to ask for her help in finding him a bride. The night she had briefly thought he was proposing to her.

It was a pretty dress, white with a purple sash and purple wisteria embroidered about the hem. But Letty hadn't been able to stand the sight of it since that horrible night. "Thank you, Sarah, but I'd rather wear—"

"You'll wear this one," her mother said, cutting her off.

Letty peered at her mother, confused. "But you hate it when I wear purple."

Her mother flicked open her fan. "Nonsense. You look lovely in purple."

Now Letty was sure she was losing her mind. "It's not even a ballgown. Surely it's not appropriate for—"

"It's your most stunning dress, and you're going to wear it," her mother said in a voice that brooked no argument.

Letty tried to protest, because honestly, just seeing the dress laid out upon her bed made her feel melancholy. But her mother and Sarah eventually managed to browbeat her into it.

Her mother stayed for the dressing process, seating herself on the bed. Which was unusual, but so long as she was there... "Mama? Might I ask for your advice?"

"Of course, darling."

Letty bit her lip. "It's just that I haven't yet decided which of my suitors to accept. If I'm being honest... I can't really imagine marrying either of them."

Her mother waved this off. "Oh, I wouldn't worry about that overly much."

Letty couldn't believe her ears. "My entire future depends upon it! Of course, I'm worried about making the right choice."

Her mother patted her hand. "I'm sure you'll figure it out, darling. All right, downstairs we go!"

Befuddled, Letty allowed her mother to shoo her down the stairs and into the crimson parlor, where she found another surprise waiting for her. "Emily? What are you doing here?"

Emily bounced on the balls of her feet. "Your mother suggested I come over. To accompany you to the Sunderland ball!"

"I—I'm sure I could use the support." It was true, but Letty couldn't quite countenance that her friend looked so giddy about the prospect.

David would be back from his trip to canvass for votes. No

doubt Emily was excited about the prospect of seeing her true love after a few days' absence.

But Letty was about as excited as if she were heading to her own funeral. For just a moment last night, after Vander had kissed her with such passion, and said he would call on her, she had allowed herself to hope that maybe *he* was going to propose.

But he hadn't come. As usual, her hopes had run away with her. Evander Beauclerk had no intentions, at least where she was concerned.

She dropped her voice down to a whisper. "Emily, the truth is... I still don't know what I'm going to do. I don't want to marry either of them, and—oh!"

She gave a start as someone seized her elbow. The scent of a familiar cinnamon-and-ginger shaving tonic washed over her.

"Vander?" she asked, turning to blink at him. And surely enough, there he was, looking heart-stoppingly handsome in his black evening kit, his hair artfully rumpled, as usual.

He smiled at her, then pressed a kiss into the palm of her hand —with her mother and father looking on!

As she stared at him, befuddled, she noticed something glinting in his cravat. It was an oval-shaped gem the size of her thumbnail, set upon a stickpin, in her very favorite color, a bright, sparkling violet.

"Vander!" she breathed. "What's that?"

He brought a hand to his cravat. "Do you mean my stickpin? It's a purple sapphire."

"It's stunning," she said, gazing at it longingly. "It's the most beautiful jewel I've ever seen."

He barked out a laugh. "I'm so pleased to hear you say that. But look at me, getting off script. I need to speak with you."

Letty frowned. "Getting off script? What do you mean—"

Ignoring her, Vander turned to Emily. "You don't mind if I steal Letty away, do you, Miss Arbuthnot?"

Emily squeezed Letty's hand, smiling broadly. "Not at all!"

Vander offered his arm to Letty. "Shall we?"

Letty looped her arm through his. "Of course. But, Vander, what are you—"

"I'll tell you in a minute. When we don't have an audience."

He led her toward the back of the house. All of this felt so familiar—the dress, Vander stealing up behind her, him taking her off alone, that she couldn't help but wonder...

But no. She had got her hopes up over Evander Beauclerk too many times before, only to be crushed when he inevitably let her down. She wasn't going to do that again.

One of their footmen, Bert, was standing at attention in the hallway, holding a tray upon which rested two glasses of champagne. Vander scooped both up in one hand without breaking stride.

He stopped just outside of her father's private study, chuckling as he realized he didn't have a free hand to open the door.

He pulled his left arm free from hers in order to reach for the knob, but Letty grabbed his hand. "Vander, wait. What are you doing?"

His smile was tender. "I'm doing it right this time."

Letty swallowed, refusing to allow herself to hope. "Doing what right? What are you—oh, my *gracious*!"

He had managed to open the door, and that was when she saw the flowers. There had to be two dozen vases of purple irises, and white rose petals scattered across the carpet.

Her heart was thundering. She had vowed not to get her hopes up. Not to get ahead of herself. *Again.*

But... this certainly *seemed* like a proposal. And, of course, she had thought that before, and it turned out to be nothing of the sort! But *surely*...

Vander shut the door behind them. Letty allowed him to guide her into one of the leather wing chairs, mouth agape, and accepted the glass of champagne he pressed into her hands.

He took the seat facing hers and smiled. "I need to ask you for a terrible favor. You see, my father is demanding that I marry."

Her hands were trembling so hard, she was afraid she would spill her champagne, so she set it down on the side table. She felt a tear slip across her cheek.

He continued, "And I was trying to think *who* I could possibly marry." They were the same words he'd spoken when they sat in this very room one week ago.

But this time, as he said, "And then, I thought of you," he rose from his seat, pulled a tiny black leather box from his pocket, and went down on one knee before her.

Now the tears were streaming down her face. She wasn't capable of forming words, so he continued, "You were actually my mother's suggestion. And as soon as I managed to pull my head out of my arse, I realized she was right."

That startled a laugh out of her. His rich brown eyes were warm as he said, "I'm jesting. At least, a little bit. But I'm not joking about this."

He flipped the box open, and she gasped. Inside lay the most beautiful ring. The center stone was identical to the one he wore in his cravat, a brilliant oval-shaped sapphire in a rich shade of lilac, surrounded by a halo of rose-cut diamonds.

He gestured to the stone at his neck. "These are sister stones. They once formed one larger gem that was split down the middle when it was found. They are perfectly matched, two halves of one whole. My mother was telling me about it today—in India, purple sapphires are believed to bring their wearer awakening and enlightenment. They help you find your life's purpose, the place where you belong."

He smiled up at her from the floor where he knelt. "It took me long enough. But I finally figured out my place. It's with you. I love you, Letty. You're my other half, the one I want to spend my life with. Will you marry me?"

"Y-yes," she sputtered, tears pouring down her face. She

laughed as she brushed her thumbs across her cheeks. "These are happy tears. I've been in love with you since I was ten."

He gave a startled laugh. "Have you really? All I needed was a chance to notice that you were no longer ten. That, and the fact that every time you tried to introduce me to someone else, I found myself wishing I was with you instead. It took me a few days, but I finally figured out what that meant."

He took her hand and slipped on the ring. Letty was so happy she thought her heart might burst.

Vander framed her face, and he was just leaning in to kiss her when the door flew open.

"Go away," he growled, glaring toward the door.

"Not a chance," his mother said, striding into the room. "Letty, darling, come here. Let me see my future daughter."

Trailing behind his mother was a crowd that included Letty's parents, Emily, and even his father. Letty was immediately surrounded, and the ladies began exclaiming over her ring.

Vander sighed. So much for having a moment to celebrate with his future bride.

He narrowed his eyes at his father as he rose from the floor. "What are *you* doing here?"

His father blinked at him from behind his spectacles. "What do you mean? It's not every day that your only son proposes marriage."

"Yes. But it's six o'clock. Shouldn't you still be at the office?"

"I've left the office at six before."

Vander arched a skeptical eyebrow. "Since when?"

His father drew himself up. "It was on the twenty-second of September, 1796."

Vander blanched. "Did you just make a *joke*?" Dear God.

Who was this man, and where was the rigid quiz he knew and loved?

His father jabbed awkwardly at Vander's arm with another one of his signature bent-wrist punches. "What can I say? I think you're rubbing off on me, son."

Over in the cluster surrounding Letty, Lady Baldridge exclaimed, "This is such a happy day. I can't wait to tell David!"

Everyone murmured agreement except for Vander. Seeing his drawn expression, the countess asked, "What is it, Vander?"

Vander shrugged. He wasn't changing his mind, regardless of whether his best friend disowned him. He would be crushed, of course, but he needed Letty in his life even more than he wanted David. "I fear David won't regard it as good news."

"He will," Emily said. "I know he will."

"You're his dearest friend," Lady Baldridge added. "How could he be anything other than thrilled?"

They didn't understand. But the only way he could explain David's true feelings would be to reveal the full extent of his former debauchery.

He didn't have the stomach for doing that, especially in front of his own mother.

So, he merely shrugged. "I'm not so sure."

Lady Baldridge clapped her hands. "Well, the servants have laid out a light dinner in the other room. Let's eat, and then we can head to Lady Sunderland's ball together."

Chapter Twenty-Five

They arrived at the Sunderland ball early. Vander scanned the ballroom for David but didn't see him.

He accompanied Letty to a deserted parlor as she met with her first two suitors, explaining that she had made her choice, and she would be marrying Vander. Lord Throckmorton took the news stoically, offering his congratulations before excusing himself.

Bertie Strickleton... not so much.

"But... but..." Bertie shot to his feet, a flailing arm knocking into a porcelain urn that began to wobble precariously. "You *have* to marry me! The fellows have already started planning my stag party. How am I going to explain to Figgy and Cheggers and Batty and Ditherington that the whole thing's off?"

Vander saw his chance to get rid of him. "You should still have your night out. It will be just the thing to cheer you. Here." He reached into his pocket and withdrew a twenty-pound banknote. "Take this. Use it to fund your bacchanalia."

Strickleton eyed the banknote. You could have a cracking good night out for twenty pounds, and although Strickleton was widely expected to come into a fortune, he didn't have it yet. Vander could tell he was tempted.

"Take it," Vander urged. "Go tonight. You'll feel better in the morning."

"All right," Strickleton said grudgingly. He cast one last mournful look at Letty. "But if you change your mind—"

"I won't," Letty said firmly. "But do enjoy yourself with your friends."

Bertie sulked out of the room, and at last, they were rid of him.

Lady Sunderland had requested that they make their announcement at the very start of the ball, so Letty could dance the opening set with her future husband. Vander went to stand next to his parents in the crowd rather than escort her to the dais, as he knew Lady Sunderland wanted to maximize the anticipation. He saw necks craning to see the ring now gracing Letty's fourth finger. Whispered speculation broke out about what man could have afforded such a spectacular piece of jewelry.

Vander glanced at his mother, who was smiling smugly. She really did have the best taste.

Vander scanned the ballroom yet again. There was still no sign of David. He knew something as simple as a muddy road or a broken wheel could have delayed his travel plans by several hours. Part of him dreaded his friend finding out that he would be the one marrying his beloved sister. But part of him just wanted to get it over with. The fallout would probably be dreadful, but at least the prospect would no longer be hanging over him like an axe.

Lady Sunderland joined Letty on the dais. She clapped her hands and the crowd fell silent. "Lady Leticia, I believe you have an announcement for us?"

"I do," Letty said, curtsying to her hostess. "I am pleased to announce that I have accepted the proposal of a fine gentleman this very afternoon."

Murmurs swept the crowd. Once they quieted, Lady Sunderland asked, "And who is the lucky gentleman who will be your bridegroom?"

Letty's eyes found his. She smiled, and for just a moment, it felt as if they were the only two people in the room. "Mr. Evander Beauclerk."

Everyone in the room started talking at once. As he threaded his way through the crowd, Beatrice Haddington Barnet, who had helped him get Letty on her own at Vauxhall, caught his eye, smiling broadly. Vander smiled back, inclining his head.

He caught snatches of conversation as he made his way to the dais—that it made sense, given the size of the ring. That they couldn't believe *he*, of all people, was settling down.

He also heard Lady Bedford whisper to her daughter that Vander was a *much* better choice than either of Letty's previous suitors. Which was nice to hear.

He joined Letty upon the dais and bowed over her hand to a smattering of applause from those assembled. When he looked up, he knew that he would never forget the way Letty was looking at him, as if she were so happy she might cry.

He rather fancied he was looking at her the same way.

He cleared his throat, offering Letty his arm. "Shall we take our places at the top of the set?"

"Let's," she said, her voice a trifle unsteady.

As Vander led her toward the three steps at the end of the dais, he spotted a familiar face toward the back of the crowd.

David had arrived.

Shit. Had David been there when Letty made her announcement? Even if he hadn't, surely he had figured it out, given that Vander was the one leading her out for the first dance.

He squinted at his friend's face as he and Letty took up their places, trying to glean a hint of his reaction. But he couldn't make out David's expression from across the ballroom.

It was a good thing the country dance was both simple and familiar because Vander's concentration was shot to hell. He tried to focus on Letty, to smile at her at every opportunity. He wanted this to be a happy memory for her.

But, if he was being honest, he was so anxious about David's reaction, he had trouble enjoying the dance.

The dance ended, and Vander bowed to Letty.

When he straightened, David was standing right there.

"So," David said.

"So," Vander replied.

They lapsed into silence. After a moment, Vander asked, "Were you here when Letty made her announcement?"

"I was," David confirmed. Another pregnant pause. Vander's neckcloth suddenly felt overly tight with his pulse pounding against it.

"Come," David finally said, "let's go someplace where we can talk. Just the two of us," he added when Vander offered his arm to Letty.

They threaded their way through the crowd and made their way to the same parlor where he and Letty had spoken to Throckmorton and Strickleton. Vander shut the door, then turned to face his fate.

David was silent, staring at the unlit fireplace. "I didn't realize you were going to propose to my sister," he finally said.

Vander rubbed the back of his head. "That makes two of us." At David's quizzical look, he added, "I only woke up and figured out I was in love with her yesterday."

David made a sound of surprise. "In love with her, are you?"

"I am," Vander said firmly. "Look, David—I know you don't want someone like me to marry your sister—"

David arched an eyebrow. "Do I not?"

"—but I'm going to be a good husband to Letty. I know I've done more than my fair share of carousing, but all of that's behind me now." His friend said nothing in reply, so after a moment, Vander added, "You probably find that hard to believe."

"Hmpf." After another awkward pause, David said, "I have only one word to say on the matter."

Vander felt as if he might be ill. This was it, the moment his friendship with David came to an end. "What's that?"

David stared at him, stony-faced, for six agonizing seconds.

Then his face split into a grin. "Finally!"

"F-finally?" Vander sputtered. He rubbed his ear, wondering if he had heard that right.

David laughed. "Yes! I've been waiting an age for you to notice that she's perfect for you. Now she's happy, you're happy, and we"—he clasped Vander by the shoulders—"are going to be brothers!"

"Thank *fuck*." Vander ran a hand over his face. "I can't believe you're happy about it. I was certain you'd call me out for even *looking* at your sister."

"So my parents were telling me." David slapped him on the shoulder, then strolled over to the sideboard in the corner and started pouring two glasses of port. "For the smartest man I know, you really are an idiot sometimes. Where on earth did you get that idea?"

David handed him his drink, and they clinked their glasses together. "It's just that you've seen me engage in some behavior that's a bit, um..."

"Degenerate?" David suggested taking a sip from his drink.

"Precisely."

"You seem to have forgotten that the reason I have observed you participating in said depraved acts is that I was right there, performing them alongside you."

"Well... yes. But I thought you would want someone a little more upright for your *sister*."

David shook his head. "You've grown up since then. I'm not going to judge you for some act of stupidity you committed when you were twenty-three. Especially when I engaged in the exact same act of stupidity."

Vander's shoulders slumped. "I'm so relieved. Here I was convinced I'd just ruined our friendship."

"No, mate." David slung an arm around his shoulders and started toward the door. "Now, if you run around behind my sister's back—"

"I won't." Vander made a slashing motion with his hand. "I know it's hard to believe, but I'm going to be a good husband to Letty."

"Course you are." David tossed back the rest of his drink and set his glass on a side table. "Besides, we both know that if you were to hurt her, I would beat you into next Tuesday."

"Fortunately for you, the point is moot, as your sister is the only one I want. Because we both know you're not capable of beating me, into next Tuesday or otherwise."

"Am so."

"Are not."

David gave him a cocky smirk. "Care to go down to Gentleman Jackson's tomorrow and settle it?"

"It happens that I would. Although we won't be boxing at Gentleman Jackson's for much longer."

David turned the knob and ushered Vander into the hallway. "Speak for yourself, old man. I've got at least another decade before they have to put me out to pasture."

Vander laughed. "That's not what I meant. There's going to be a new boxing venue opening in the parish of St. George in the East, which I think you're going to find you prefer."

They had reached Letty, who was chatting with a handful of well-wishers including Emily. David squeezed Vander's shoulder, then released him. "St. George in the East, you say? Color me intrigued."

David wandered over to talk to his own future bride. Vander came to stand beside Letty.

After a few minutes, the musicians started tuning up again. "Dance with me," he murmured in her ear.

She gave him a sideways look. "I'm not sure that it's proper for us to dance twice in a row. And if you claim this dance, it will be our last one for the night, as it's not permissible for us to dance more than two times."

Vander was already leading her toward the ballroom floor. "Ah, yes. If we dance more than twice, we'll have to marry. Say... how many times do I have to dance with you for your parents to insist that we marry *tomorrow*?"

"Van-der. Are you trying to cause a scandal?"

"Don't be absurd. Were I trying to cause a scandal, I would do this," he said, snagging two glasses of champagne off of a passing waiter's tray, then steering Letty straight past the dancers forming into a set and toward the French doors that led to the balcony.

She tutted, but she was smiling as she let him lead her out onto the balcony. She accepted a glass. "Come, Vander. You can cause a bigger scandal than that."

"I could," he agreed, clinking his glass against hers. "I'm tempering myself, as I'll soon be a respectable married man."

There was a gleam in Letty's eye as she set her glass on the stone balustrade. A gleam that looked... promising. "What's the fun in that? There's a reason I'm marrying a notorious rake."

Much to Vander's delight, she looped her arms around his neck and pulled his head down for a kiss, right there in full view of the ballroom.

Indeed, a number of Lady Sunderland's guests spotted them and were duly scandalized.

But only in the best possible way.

Epilogue

May 1821
One Year Later

They called it a grand opening, although that wasn't really true.

The new offices of Beauclerk Marine Casualty had been in use for the last month. But Vander had convinced his father that it was worthwhile to host a formal celebration to which everyone, including the press, could be invited. It would show the world that they were a serious player in the insurance industry. Appearances were important.

Vander's father had agreed without much argument. He'd come to trust his son on these sorts of things.

David was the one to escort Letty to the office as Vander had to be there early. He brought Emily, too.

The new Lady Trundley peered around the coffee house that took up half of the ground floor. "This is fascinating! I've never been allowed to visit a coffee house before."

David placed a hand on the small of his wife's back and guided her toward the stairs. "You should not linger in this one."

"Couldn't I stay just for a few minutes?" Emily asked. "I might need to write a scene that takes place in a coffee house someday."

Letty's friend had moved on from obsessively reading Gothic novels to attempting to write her own. It wasn't a proper pursuit for a future countess, but David didn't care. He was well and truly besotted and would've encouraged Emily to join the circus, had the spirit moved her.

"Besides," Emily continued, "I'm sure the Beauclerks run a respectable establishment."

"Sailors, Emily," David said. "Most of the men in here are sailors."

"That makes me want to stay even more!" Emily protested as David herded her toward the back stairs.

Letty, looking beautiful in a violet spencer over a white dress, peered around the coffee house, as curious as her friend. It was plain but inviting, with oak-paneled walls. The tables were starting to show their first scratches, but it didn't bother Vander. It wasn't a bad thing that the room felt lived in.

Her brown eyes were bright as she turned to him. "It's wonderful, Vander," she whispered.

It truly was. With Lloyd's having abandoned their coffee house for an office in the Royal Exchange Building, Beauclerk Marine Casualty's new coffee house had become the place for everyone from ship owners to sea captains to gather. And they had more than just a coffee house—at Vander's suggestion, a fencing-parlor-slash-boxing-school had also been installed on the ground floor. A fencing master came in on Monday, Wednesday, and Friday, and a boxing instructor on Tuesday, Thursday, and Saturday. Every sea captain fancied himself a man of action—even the ones who were octogenarians—and the fencing parlor had proved a very popular addition. Between that and the coffee house, Beauclerk Marine Casualty was now *the* place to go if you were in the shipping business, and his father never had cause to complain that he was the last one to hear the latest gossip.

Vander offered Letty his arm. Leaning down close to her ear, he asked, "How are you feeling?"

She smiled up at him. "I'm well this morning."

He studied her face to see if it was true. "The motion of the carriage didn't make you feel ill?"

They had found out two weeks ago that the Beauclerk family was about to undergo an expansion. Which was unsurprising, given how much time they'd dedicated to the sorts of activities that led to this happy event.

"Truly, I'm fine," she reassured him.

"All right." He led her toward the stairs in the back. "Come, I'll show you the rest of it."

On the top floor, he led his wife through the open floor space where the clerks had their desks. Across the back wall were three offices, all confusingly labeled *Mr. Beauclerk* with only an initial to distinguish between the three partners. Strictly speaking, the name of the business was now Beauclerk, Beauclerk, and Beauclerk Marine Casualty.

"Milton's office is in that corner," Vander said, pointing. "My father has the big office in the middle. And this"—he opened the door to the right corner office—"is mine."

Letty gasped as she entered the room where Vander spent much of his days. Sunlight poured in through the tall windows lining two walls. There was a fine view of the bustling port where ships were being loaded and unloaded.

"Vander," she breathed, "this is *wonderful*."

It really was, and he was surprised how easily he'd settled into his new routine. Each day, he would spend an hour or so boxing or fencing. David even made a point of coming there to box a few times a week, so he even got to spend time with his friend. He would also go downstairs and have a coffee whenever he needed a break. These were things he enjoyed, but they were also good opportunities to 'gather intelligence,' as his father put it, a term that really just meant talking to people.

Well, Vander was good at talking to people, even if his father wasn't.

He spent most of his workday performing mathematical analysis in his sunlit office, in particular overseeing the high-risk insurance pool he had originated. It had performed well in its first year and had doubled in size for this sailing season.

He was usually done by three o'clock. He could take his wife for a drive in the park or meet David at the club for a drink. Or he could just relax at home with Letty before they headed out for the evening's entertainment.

He had plenty of time to do the things he enjoyed, and he felt good about himself. He never would've believed it a year ago, but his new life as a partner in Beauclerk Marine Casualty suited him tremendously.

The reason Vander was able to maintain such a reasonable work schedule poked his head into his office. "I heard Mrs. Beauclerk was here."

"Come in, Milton," Vander said. It had been Vander's idea to officially make Milton a partner and offer him a stake in the business. Milton might never be great at tallying up rows of figures, but his contribution was invaluable. He now performed all of the office management and supervisory types of tasks, leaving Vander free to focus on mathematical analysis. The cousins complemented each other, and Vander's joke that together, he and Milton made one fully functioning person had proved to be prescient.

Even more surprising than the fact that his father had agreed to all of these changes was how much his father liked this new setup. He had always been resistant to delegating any of his tasks. But Vander somehow convinced him to agree to a one-month trial of Milton running the office. When he realized how much time this freed up for him to spend analyzing policies, he had quickly grown to appreciate the change.

With Vander also performing analysis and his father wasting less time on mundane tasks, they'd been able to increase the size of the business by sixty percent last year. The coffee house was making a profit which just about offset the increased cost of their better offices.

Vander still caught his father recoiling in shock upon occasion, usually when a cloud receded and actual sunlight fell upon his face. But he admitted that the changes Vander had implemented had been for the best.

A clerk stepped into the room. "Excuse, me, Mr. Beauclerk?" he said to Milton. "Miss Seymour has arrived."

It had been Vander's idea to introduce his cousin to Mathilda Seymour, the lovely but demure young lady Letty had tried to match him with at the British Museum. Milton might only have a ten percent stake in Beauclerk Marine Casualty, but that was enough to make him a wealthy man. As Vander had suspected, the modest Miss Seymour had been charmed by his strait-laced cousin, and the two were to be married next month.

Milton excused himself to go greet his future bride, leaving Vander alone with his wife.

Vander stole up behind Letty, who was enjoying the view of the bustling port, wrapping his arms around her waist. Leaning down, he murmured in her ear, "If there weren't so many people milling about, your rakish husband would show you some enjoyable things we can do on that desk."

Laughing, Letty turned around, twining her fingers in his hair. "My rakish husband has already shown me those things in the library at home. Several times, might I add. But if you put your spectacles on, you just might be able to convince me."

Vander chuckled as he buried his nose in Letty's hair. This had been yet another revelation from the past year—that Letty liked him just as well when he was wearing his spectacles, up to his eyeballs in figures, acting like, dare he say it, a quiz. He didn't have to maintain some rake-about-town facade, to hide who he really was, because she liked him as he really was.

How had he ever tolerated his old life? His new one was infinitely better.

He pressed a kiss against her forehead before leaning back. "Is there anything else you want to see before we go?"

She rumpled his hair, getting it just the way she liked it. "It happens that there is. I am given to understand that there is a boxing school on the ground floor. One year ago, the Brazen Belle brought to my attention the fact that just about every other woman in England had enjoyed the sight of the man I pined after engaged in bare-chested fisticuffs. But, alas, I have still never witnessed these delights."

Vander grinned. "Well, we can't have that. So long as you don't mind the sight of your brother getting pummeled, I will be happy to oblige you."

"Really?" Letty looked surprised as well as delighted. "I was worried you would tell me no, that you would say it would start a scandal."

"Oh, it will." He gave her his charming scoundrel's smile as he offered her his arm. "Let's start this one together."

He and Letty headed down the stairs arm-in-arm, toward all the adventures their future held.

Keep reading for a special preview of Book Six in The Rake Review series, *The Scot Who Made June Hot* by Fenna Edgewood!

Looking for a place to discuss all of your favorite rakes? Check out the Brazen Belles Facebook Group! You'll find games, giveaways, and a place to connect with historical romance authors and readers. We hope you'll join us!

I write a free bonus story for each of my books, exclusively for my newsletter subscribers. The bonus story for *One Fine May* features Vander's sweet-but-bumbling cousin, Milton, and tells the story of his meet-cute with Mathilda. If you choose to subscribe, you'll receive updates from me about twice a month with Regency fun, all my latest news, and the occasional video of me starting a fire whilst dabbling in historical cooking. You can sign up at courtneymccaskill.com/newsletter .

Preview: The Scot Who Made June Hot

Coming Soon:

Book 6 in The Rake Review series, *The Scot Who Made June Hot* by Fenna Edgewood

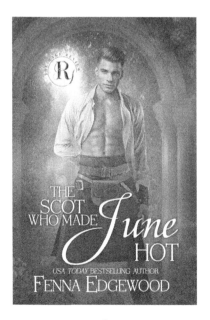

A Second Chance She Doesn't Want...

Lady June Fairchild has a terrible secret. Before she became the wife of an esteemed earl, she was married once before... and her husband was never officially confirmed dead.

Now, nearly ten years later, the unimaginable has happened. Her first husband has returned--and he wants her back. The only problem? Lady June has no intention of going anywhere with this handsome, bitter stranger.

From Out of the Shadows of Betrayal...

The night after he was handfasted to the woman he pledged to love for a lifetime, Cameron Fraser was forced to disappear into the night. Upon his return, he learned his new bride had not waited around but instead had married an earl just a few weeks later, becoming a brazen bigamist.

Now, ten years later, this jilted, kilted Highland husband has returned to greet his bride and this time he won't be keeping his presence a secret. He's a grown man and he's ready to take back what's his, come hell or high water.

Can two hearts bound by fate and torn apart by secrets find a way to trust and love once more?

CHAPTER 1

Windermere Manor, June 1820

Summer had arrived. The sky was blue and bright sunshine streamed down from overhead.

Lady June Fairchild sat on a window seat watching one of the children from the Dower House play on the lawn below. They really were beautiful children, she thought, as she ran the ivory comb through her long yellow hair. With their mother's dark coloring and charming smile, how could they not be?

She looked at the sky again. The many days of rain seemed to have abated. Perhaps it would be a beautiful summer after all.

A small flicker of hope was rising in her chest as she thought of the season ahead, one filled with walks in the sun and... The door to the dressing chamber was pushed open and then slammed.

Her husband had entered. Only the earl would not bother to close his countess's door softly behind him.

He wished to announce his presence to her. To enter abruptly and with a bang. It gave him pleasure to try to startle her in even a small way.

It took some self-restraint but she managed not to turn. Simply kept brushing the comb through her hair.

"Where is your maid? Should you not be ready by now?" He was already annoyed. Something else must have gone wrong and he had come here to take it out on her. Well, it would not be the first time nor the last. A pause. "Is that what you're wearing? Have you nothing else?"

She made herself turn, slowly, to face him and smile reassuringly. "It is only one o'clock, John."

"And our guests are due to arrive by five and you must be there to greet them," he snapped.

She took a breath, trying for patience, fighting the urge to argue. It was pointless with John. She had learned that long ago. Or if not pointless, entirely unworth the pain and sorrow. And so she suppressed the instinct to inform him that it did not take her longer than half an hour to dress and that if he did not like the gown she had chosen, he might choose another or perhaps blame himself, for many of her clothes were older and he had seen them before. If he did not like this fact, he might increase her allowance. But she knew it was dangerous to suggest this for the estate was impoverished–and besides, she did not really give a fig about how many dresses she had or how old they were. Only, John did. And he wanted her to care–even though she could not do anything about it one way or another.

"I will be ready," she said, keeping her voice calm. "I promise you."

"Dinner must go perfectly," the Earl of Windermere said. He looked at the pale blue muslin frock hanging near the wardrobe and frowned. "I suppose it will do."

"I hope so," June murmured, casting her eyes downwards.

"That is not what I came to speak to you about, in any case."

Her heart raced. His voice had turned colder. Not a good sign. She had hoped he would depart. Now it seemed he meant to stay.

"Oh? Is it about dinner? You approved the menu last week and I thought it was agreeable to you..."

"Not the damned dinner." He lifted his hand and now she saw it was not empty. A piece of folded paper was in it. He waved it and his face darkened red.

"Have you seen this, Wife?" he demanded. He preferred to address her as such. It was a way, she believed, of removing even more of her sense of self. Of making her feel even less an individual. She was not June to him. Simply wife. A role that any woman might have filled.

But only she had been stupid enough to do so.

"I do not believe so. But then," she said reasonably. "I do not know what it is. The Times, I suppose?"

He gave a cruel laugh that she knew was meant to intimidate her and stepped closer to where she sat by the window. "Not the Times."

She shrank back a little. "Nothing upsetting, I hope. I know how much you are looking forward to this house party."

"Looking forward to it?" His eyes narrowed. "Everything rests upon this event's success. Everything."

"I know you are hoping to capture the Duke of Tulloch's interest in your investments," June said softly. "I assure you, I will do everything in my power to ensure things go as smoothly as possible."

"Oh?" the earl responded frostily. "You will, will you?" He stepped up beside the window seat and dropped the piece of paper beside her like a hot coal. "And yet already this household is embroiled in the most sordid gossip. All because of you."

Her heart hammering, she reached for the folded paper and opened it carefully.

Dearest Reader,

As the summer sun casts its warm embrace upon the English countryside, a new arrival has stirred the simmering cauldron of London gossip. The object of our fascination? None other than the dashing Duke of T–, who, like a Highland breeze, has swept into our midst from the misty moors.

Ah, but dear readers, let us not be deceived by the noble title bestowed upon him, for the Duke of T– is renowned far and wide for his exploits as a beguiling rake. While some may claim to be put off by his fiery red locks and freckled countenance which mark the duke as a true son of Caledonia, let us assure you that tales of his amorous conquests have traveled from the cobbled streets of Edinburgh to the bustling salons of London, where whispers of his captivating brogue and strapping tartan-clad presence precede him like the herald of a tempest.

But it is not only the ladies of London who may find themselves ensnared by the Duke of T–'s irresistible charm. Nay, even the most steadfast of matrons should beware, for his reputation as a rake of unparalleled skill knows no bounds.

And yet, what whisper is this in my ear? May the hunter yet become the hunted?

This very week, the Duke of T– shall make his way from London to the sleepy countryside to pay a visit to the Earl of W–'s fine estate. Not only may the Duke of T– find much to admire in the splendid scenery, but a lady who is said to epitomize the season will be waiting for him there: Lady J– F–, the Countess of W–, with her golden tresses reminiscent of a hot summer's day and her light blue eyes that are said to sparkle like a beautiful loch. Will she prove to be the duke's next conquest?

Or do we underestimate this particular matron? Could it be that Lady J– will be the trap that finally ensnares this Scottish rake? Whispers of the lovely lady's own scandalous past have begun to emerge this Season. Rumors of a dalliance with a young man of questionable reputation, before she was whisked away to the country-side again by her notoriously jealous husband.

Ah, dear readers, the plot thickens and the stage is set. Let us watch with bated breath as the Duke of T– and Lady J– dance ever closer to the edges of scandal and ruin.

Until next we meet, I remain
Yours in Brazen Speculation,
The Belle

June felt her face flush as if with fever. She glanced up at her husband.

"I've never even met the Duke of Tulloch. You know that. And as for this terrible bit of slander about last Season, you know for a fact I was helping the Baron of Granville's son through a fit of asthma that overcame him while we were dancing."

"Yes, and were found secluded with him in an empty room at a ball," the earl said frostily.

"Found by the physician who was called to attend to poor Alexander," June exclaimed, feeling her cheeks become even hotter. A physician with a malicious wagging tongue. Curse the man. Alexander had been choking and gasping for air and all she had been trying to do was get him to a quiet place so that he might catch his breath. She had been doing no more than leaning over him and patting his back–like his own mother might have done. Why, the boy was no more than seventeen years of age. A mere child compared to her own twenty-eight years!

"I did nothing his own mother would not have done," she said, repeating her thoughts desperately. "And his parents thanked me for it, as you may recall."

"I recall you making a perfect fool of yourself," her husband said. "And having to escort you from London before you could do anything even more ridiculous before the entire ton."

This was pointless, she saw, her heart sinking. He wanted her to feel humiliated. There was never any point in arguing with John. And yet the horrible thing was that he wanted her to argue. He wanted her to contradict him. As if he knew that in her heart, she was doing so constantly.

"I was only trying to help," she said quietly. "And I have no intention of making you ridiculous in front of any of your guests."

"No? And yet this Duke of Tulloch sounds like a fine fellow. A handsome rake, they say." The Earl of Windermere sneered. "Despite his being no better than a barbarian. Like all the Scots. Edinburgh, indeed. Tulloch's seat is far from any sign of civilization from what I am given to understand."

Ah, so this was not really about her at all but about John's concerns to do with the duke. A man with a more elevated title, a larger estate, and, from what John had already let slip, far more money to run it with. Which was precisely why her husband hoped to trick the Scotsman into parting with some of his riches and funding poor, increasingly-dilapidated Windermere.

"I will stay far away from the duke, if that is what you wish," she offered. She thought of dinner. "It's not too late to alter the seating arrangements. I can..."

"Enough." The earl's voice cut through her words. "What I wish is for you to be..."

He paused and she could almost hear him thinking. What he wanted was for her to be just charming enough, just winsome enough, just flirtatious enough to enchant the duke. For in doing so, the duke might just be more willing to listen to John's ridiculous schemes for opening a mine on the Windermere estate, funded, of course, almost solely by the duke himself. There was only so much brandy and whiskey one could ply a man with. And if the duke had a good head on his shoulders, liquor would not be enough.

But place a woman in front of him—and that might do the trick.

"You wish for me to be a charming hostess but to know my place," June said dully. "I understand, John. I really do."

The earl's eyes flashed. "You have never known your place."

"I have always been a loyal and submissive wife," she retorted before she could help herself. "Which is more than one could ever say for you as a husband."

There it was. She saw the gleam of victory in his eyes.

And then his hand was raising and swiftly descending.

He had won and she had lost. The proof was in the pain.

The Duke of Tulloch had arrived at the Earl of Windermere's house party earlier than expected.

Anticipating a rainy day like the ones preceding, he had been surprised by the appearance of sun. With warm conditions to dry out the roads, his carriage had made much better time.

And hence he found himself arriving at Windermere Manor earlier than his hosts had anticipated him.

Leaving his luggage with the servants, he had refused offers to be shown to his room or to have his hosts called down to greet him. Instead, he had marched out onto the lawn, intending to take a constitutional before returning and greeting his hosts and fellow guests before dinner.

Yet as he crossed the green manor lawn, a gazebo came into view and he saw he was not the first guest to arrive after all.

A woman was seated inside the small, octagonal pavilion with her back to him. Around her on either side, delicate columns supported a latticed roof covered with climbing roses and trailing vines.

The woman sat upon a cushioned bench, her slender form draped in a pale blue muslin gown that billowed softly in the breeze. Though her features were obscured by the shadows cast by the lattice, the curve of her shoulders and the graceful lines of her figure spoke to an innate elegance and poise.

Deciding it would be more fitting to leave the woman to her solitary contemplation than for a strange man to interrupt, the duke began to step quietly around the gazebo.

The faint sound of weeping echoed from the gazebo.

Glancing once more towards the little pavilion, he realized the woman's slender shoulders were trembling with sobs. Her delicate hands clutched the fabric of her gown.

Swearing imperceptibly to himself, the duke paused. He could leave the lady in peace or he could see if she required aid.

Chances were high she was crying over nothing more than a stain on her dress or a broken vase. These highborn women often seemed to care of little more than their material comforts. Tulloch did not have high hopes that the guests at Windermere's house party would be any different than the countless women he had met before. Especially one in particular.

Still, this was a woman and she could well be in real distress.

With a gentle clearing of his throat, Tulloch stepped forward, allowing the soft crunch of gravel beneath his boots to alert the lady to his presence and give her a moment to prepare.

As expected, he caught the sound of a gasp. The woman lifted her head, looking at first not at him but straight in front of her. And in that moment, he caught sight of two things.

The lady's tear-stained cheek was to be expected. After all, she had been crying.

What the duke had not expected to see and, aye, what he despised, was the sight of the ugly red welt marking the lady's otherwise unblemished lily-white features.

"Who did that to ye, lass? Who struck ye?" He spoke sharply and without thinking, anger already welling up inside of him. Injustice had always infuriated him. Even as a small boy he had begun fights he had not been able to win, simply because he had been compelled to by a stubborn sense of conscience.

He had reached the gazebo steps now. The woman had not replied.

"Tell me, lass, and I swear, I'll thrash the man within an inch of his life," Tulloch promised. "There's never a call for a man to lay a hand on a woman. Tell me who the blackguard was and he'll learn this as he should have long ago. He'll nay harm ye again."

The woman turned her head towards him, and as she did so a beam of light fell upon her hair.

The lady's hair was not brown as he had assumed. No, it was the shade of a field of wheat on a hot summer's day. Golden and lush.

He felt his throat go dry. This woman was no guest. She was the lady of the manor.

More than that–she was the woman he had married ten long years ago.

Tulloch swore aloud.

～

The Scot Who Made June Hot will be available on June 1, 2024. Pre-order your copy today!

Historical Note

A few of my early readers expressed surprise that Vander and his mother speak Persian. Although Persian is not much spoken in India today, during the eighteenth and early nineteenth centuries, it was one of two lingua francas on the Indian subcontinent, along with Hindustani (as it was called by English speakers during the nineteenth century). What's more, according to an analysis performed by Professor Michael H. Fisher, a strong majority of Indians who emigrated to Britain during the eighteenth and nineteenth centuries were native speakers of Persian. It therefore made the most sense for Vander and his mother to speak Persian, even though this may seem like a surprising choice to modern readers. The use of Persian in India began to decline during the mid-nineteenth century.

I would like to mention some of the real Anglo-Indians I came across in doing my research, who inspired me as I was thinking about what Vander's life might have been like in Regency England.

William and Kitty Kirkpatrick were the children of James Achilles Kirkpatrick, who served as the British Resident for the East India Company in Hyderabad, and Indian noblewoman

Khair un-Nissa. They were born in India but sent to England upon their father's death. Both received a significant inheritance from their father.

William suffered a childhood injury involving boiling water that was severe enough that one of his arms had to be amputated. He led something of a quiet life as a result of these injuries, but he still managed to attend Oxford, marry, and have three daughters before his untimely death at the age of twenty-seven.

His sister, Kitty, did not lead a quiet life; she was a society darling. Regarded as a great beauty and widely rumored to be the daughter of an "Indian Princess," Kitty achieved fame as the muse of author Thomas Carlyle. The character Blumine in his popular novel *Sartor Resartus* was said to be inspired by Kitty. She married a dashing army officer, James Winslowe Phillipps, with whom she had seven children. Based on their letters, the marriage appears to have been a happy one.

For more information about William and Kitty, I can enthusiastically recommend the excellently researched book *White Mughals* by William Dalrymple.

Fewer details are known about the life of Thomas Deane Mahomet Pearse, son of Thomas Deane Pearse and Punna Purree Pearse. But we do know that he attended Harrow and later Oriel College, Oxford in the late eighteenth century.

Katherine Scott Forbes was the daughter of Scotsman Theodore Forbes and the housekeeper he hired while living in Surat, Eliza Kewark. Thanks to DNA testing, we know that Eliza was Indian. (We can say this with precision because some of the genetic markers in question were found on her descendants' mitochondrial DNA, which is always passed down from mother to child. We therefore know that these particular genes trace down the maternal line).

Katherine and her descendants must have either mixed in fashionable circles or made a precipitous climb up the social ladder because a few generations later, her great-great-granddaughter, the Honourable Frances Ruth Roche, married Edward John Spencer, the Eighth Earl Spencer.

These two happen to be the parents of Princess Diana, meaning that the future King of England, Prince William, and his brother, Prince Harry, have Anglo-Indian ancestry.

Finally, a mea culpa! As I'm sure everyone *immediately* noticed, the Woodhousian Method of Graduation with regards to Mortality Tables dates to 1888, not 1820! Rest assured, had Mr. Woodhouse proposed his controversial methods in 1820, Vander's father would have been thoroughly scandalized.

I would like to thank my fabulous editor, Diana Bold; my indispensable beta readers Ritika and Linda; and my cover designer, Dar Albert, who is both brilliant and extremely patient. I'd like to thank all of my author and reader friends in The Brazen Belles! Y'all make this crazy author life so much more enjoyable. I am also so grateful for the members of my ARC and street teams, especially Melinda who creates order out of chaos. The most thanks, of course, goes to my wonderful family, especially J and V. I love you two to the moon and back!

This one is for one of my favorite people on the face of this earth. This one is for Eddie!

More Books by Courtney McCaskill

The Astley Chronicles Series
How to Train Your Viscount
What's an Earl Gotta Do?
The Sea Siren of Broadwater Bottom
The Duke's Dark Secret
My Favorite Mistake: An Astley Chronicles Novella
Let Me Be Your Hero (2024)
Romancing the Rifleman (2025)

The Weatherby Wallflowers Series
A Wallflower Never Surrenders (2024)
Snowbound with the Scoundrel (2024)
One Bed for the Bluestocking (2025)
How He Won His Wallflower (2025)

The Wicked Widows' League
Scoundrel for Sale
A Very Roguish Boxing Day (2024)
An Officer and a Rakehell (2025)

About the Author

After reading *Black Beauty* for the 1,497th time, Courtney McCaskill was inspired to write her own stories. Reviews of her early work were mixed, with her fourth-grade teacher, Mrs. Compton, saying, "Please stop writing all of your essays from the point of view of a horse."

Today, Courtney lives in Austin, Texas with the hero of her own story, who holds the distinction of being the world's most sarcastic pediatrician. She is reliably informed by her son that she gives THE BEST hugs, "because you're so squishy, Mommy." In 2022, Regency Fiction Writers honored her with its Lady of the Realm award in appreciation of her volunteer work, both on its Board of Directors and as the Coordinator of the Regency Academe. When she's not busy almost burning her house down while attempting to make a traditional Christmas pudding, she enjoys playing the piano, learning everything there is to know about Kodiak bears, and of course, curling up with a great book. Visit her online at www.courtneymccaskill.com.

Made in United States
Orlando, FL
05 June 2024

47566016R00125